REMINISCENCES

OF AN

OLD TEACHER.

By GEORGE B. EMERSON.

1878.

INTRODUCTION.

AFTER much hesitation I have concluded, notwithstanding the advice of some of my best friends, to reprint from the *Journal of Education* some of the papers which I furnished, at the editor's request, as Reminiscences of an Old Teacher. I should be glad to have every young man in the country seeking for a truly liberal education live such a life as I lived till I entered college. Through life, though spent at a distance from the fields, and in an occupation as unlike husbandry and gardening as possible, I have enjoyed the familiar knowledge I obtained of the earth, and of everything that grows out of the earth, and of the animals, quadrupeds, birds, fishes, and insects with which I became familiarly acquainted. I have been benefited and blest by the habits I formed of using all my bodily faculties in daily vigorous exercise for some hours every summer's day till I entered college.

CONTENTS.

REMINISCENCES

OF AN

OLD TEACHER.

CHAPTER I.

I YIELD to your request so far as to give you some account of certain years of my life, because I think there are things to be told which may be of use to other teachers. I was born on the 12th of September, 1797, in Wells, in the county of York, district of Maine, then a part of Massachusetts. My father, a native of Hollis, New Hampshire, and a graduate of Cambridge in 1784, was a physician, a man of cultivation and taste, an excellent Latin scholar, well read in history and especially in old English poetry, a good story-teller, and a most agreeable companion. These qualities made him very attractive.

The Supreme Court of Massachusetts had two circuits every year into Maine, the judges travelling in their own carriages, and holding a court at York and at Portland. The best tavern between these towns was Jefferds's, a short distance from my father's house, and the judges usually spent a night there. As they became acquainted with my father, they often passed an evening at his house, and I thus had the good fortune to become acquainted with such men as Judge Jackson and

1

the reporter, Dudley Atkins Tyng, — gentlemen distinguished for their character and ability, and no less for
the simplicity and refinement of their manners.

As my father was a person of great public spirit, he
was usually chairman of the school committee, and took
care that there should always be a well-educated man
as master of the school. Notwithstanding its excellence, my elder brother and myself were always, after I
reached the age of eight years, kept at home and set to
work as early in the season as there was anything to be
done in the garden or on our little farm. I thus gradually became acquainted with sowing, weeding, and har-
vesting, and with the seeds, the sprouting and growth
of all the various roots and stems and blossoms. I
naturally watched the character, shape, and structure of
the roots and of the leaves, the formation of the blossoms, their flowering, the calyx, the petals, their times
of opening, coming to perfection, persistence or falling,
and the successive changes in the seed-vessels till the
maturity of the seed, of all the plants of the garden and
the field. I became also familiarly acquainted with all
the weeds and their roots, and the modes of preventing
their doing harm. I was getting real knowledge of
things ; I formed the habit of observing. This was
always valuable knowledge, the use of which I felt afterwards when I began to study botany as a science, and
as long as I pursued it ; for, reading the description of
a plant, I saw not the words of the book, but the roots
and stems and leaves and flowers and seeds of the plant
itself. And this habit of careful observation I naturally
extended to whatever was the subject of my reading or
study.

This was valuable, but I made another attainment of still greater value. I learned how to use every tool, spade and shovel, hoe, fork, rake, knife, sickle, and scythe, and to like to use them. I learned the use of all my limbs and muscles, and to enjoy using them. Labor was never, then nor afterwards, a hardship. I was not confined to the garden and field. I had to take care of horses, cows, sheep, and fowls, and early learned their character and habits, and that to make them all safe and kind and fond of me, it was only necessary to be kind to them. My father's garden extended from the house some little distance down to the river Mousum, a stream which issued from a lake more than thirty miles above, and furnished in its course motive-power to many saw-mills and grist-mills, two of which, and the mill-· ponds which supplied them, were less than a quarter of a mile below our garden ; and up to the lower one came the tide from the sea.

My brother and I were never obliged to work hard, nor for more than four or five hours a day, except in times of exigency, such as the threatening of rain when the made hay was on the ground. We were led, and opportunity was given, to become acquainted with the woods and streams and the sea. We were often told by our father that if we would make certain beds or squares perfectly clean, by such a day, we should go with him to Cape Porpoise, to fish for cunners and rock-cod, to Little Harbor for sea-trout, or up or down the Mousum for pickerel or perch. I thus became gradually acquainted with the fresh-water fishes above the dams, and those of salt water below, — an attainment of great value when I became responsible for the accuracy of

volumes of Natural History submitted to my oversight.

We were allowed, at the proper seasons, on similar
conditions, to join our sisters, in summer, in gathering
huckleberries or blueberries, on Picwacket Plain, where
they grew, as they now grow, in the greatest luxuriance.
In the fall, we went up the Mousum to gather chestnuts,
over to Harrasicket for shagbarks, along the edges of
the fields nearer home for hazel-nuts, and to the nearer
and sometimes the more distant fields for strawberries,
blackberries, and raspberries.

Early in the morning I drove, or rather accompanied,
the cows to pasture, half a mile off, and led them back
at night. I rode the horses to water, and often har-
nessed and unharnessed them. I have, through life,
found it a great advantage to know how to do these
things, and to be able to do them speedily and readily
myself.

I had constant opportunities, at all seasons of the
year, of becoming acquainted with the trees and shrubs
of the neighborhood, — the oaks, beech, birches, maples,
hickories, pines, spruces, fir, and hemlock, and many of
the shrubs and flowers. My father told me what sta-
mens and pistils were, and that, according to the number and position of these, Linnæus had arranged all
plants into classes and orders. Mr. John Low, a near
neighbor of ours, lent me the first volume of the
" Memoirs of the American Academy," containing Dr.
Manassah Cutler's account of the vegetable produc-
tions growing near Ipswich, Mass. From this, with
some other helps, I became acquainted with many,
indeed most of the flowers and other wild plants in

our neighborhood, all, at least, that Dr. Cutler had
described.*

With all these pursuits, my brother and I had hours,
almost every day, and the whole of rainy days, for reading and study. I read, with interest, books of travels,
— Carver's and Bartram's, Park's travels in Africa, and
Bruce's. I read much of the old poetry of our language, — Chaucer's, Surrey's, Drayton's, and still more
of Cowper, Thomson, Goldsmith, Milton, Young, Gray,
and others. With what delight did we devour the "Lay
of the Last Minstrel," and all of Scott's poems as they
came out!

My brother was then reading Virgil, and I perfectly
remember one day when my father came into our room
to hear him recite his lesson. I got leave to remain.
My brother read, —

"Infandum, regina, jubes renovare dolorem" (*Æn.* II, 3);

and translated, "Immense grief, O queen, you command me to renew." "No, my dear boy, that is not
a translation. Observe that *infandum* is from *for*, *fari*,
to speak, with the negative *in*. 'Immense' is no translation of that word. Indeed, it is a Latin word, and
therefore no translation of any word. *Immensus* means
unmeasured. 'Immense' is no translation. Then
dolorem does not mean grief. Æneas felt not grief for
what he had suffered: it gave him pain to call it to
mind. Then Queen Dido was treating Æneas with the
greatest attention and respect. She would not com-

---

* Dr. Cutler's account of "Indigenous Vegetables" is one of the
most valuable papers ever given to American botanists. It is richly
worth study even now.

mand him ; she bade him, as we bid one another, ' Good morning,' or to come to dinner. The proper translation is, ' Unutterable pain, O queen, thou bidst me to renew.' "

I then knew scarcely a word of Latin, but I always remembered this lesson as the best lesson I ever learned. I was immediately possessed by the idea and desire of studying Latin, and asked my father to let me begin. This he did, and set me to˙ study Erasmus, Corderius, and others of the old school-books of seventy or eighty or a hundred years ago. He did not set me to commit to memory anything in grammar, but only to find out for myself the cases of nouns and adjectives, and the moods and tenses of verbs. In this way I went through some volumes of prose, and Virgil and parts of Ovid in poetry, though I read these with care and thoroughly. He let me go through the Greek Testament in a similar way, but declined to let me go on, as he distrusted his own knowledge of the Greek language, though I have no doubt, from his remembering and often quoting so many of the best lines in Sappho and Homer, that he might have done it with success.

When the last ear of corn was husked and the last potato in the cellar, I went back to school. The other boys, my cousins and playmates, had been in school all summer, and were tired of it. I went back with delight, and gave myself to the work earnestly and diligently. Thus, though I was behind the others in my studies, I resumed and pursued them with so much zeal that I soon placed myself above many older, and brighter naturally than myself.

So great were the advantages of my summer's employments that I have, for many years, had no doubt that it would be far better for all the boys in the country towns of Massachusetts not to be allowed to go to school in the summer, but to educate their muscles and form habits of observation and industry by pursuits similar to those which it was my privilege and happiness to be engaged in.

I was sent to Dummer Academy, in Byfield, where I remained twelve or fourteen weeks, and learned to repeat perfectly all that was required of Adam's Latin Grammar and the Gloucester Greek. What made it easy was that I knew so much of the languages as instantly to understand what many of the poor fellows there had early committed to memory, of much of the meaning of which they had no idea. This experience was valuable to me, but what was still more so was the acquaintance formed with boys whom I met afterwards at Cambridge, with some of whom I opened a correspondence which lasted as long as they lived.

- CHAPTER II.

NEXT to my father's house dwelt Major Cozens, a quiet man, who had been a major in the old French war. His mode of life was of the primitive type. His land lay next my father's garden and fields, which had been purchased of him. He culti-vated Indian corn, potatoes, peas, and beans, and other vegetables, and flax, which he carried through all the processes of rotting, breaking, combing, and clean-ing, till it was ready, in its two forms of flax and tow, for the little wheel of his wife and the large wheels of his daughters and granddaughter. They spun, and, in the winter, their father wove their spinning into the linen and tow-cloth for the pillow-cases and sheets, and tablecloths and towels, of the family. The Major also kept a flock of sheep large enough to furnish food for the family and for sale, and all the wool wanted for the warmer garments of the family, which the mother and daughters spun, and the father wove. For the few things to be made of cotton, this was bought at the shops, and carded and spun and woven at home.

They kept several cows, furnishing them abundance of milk, butter, and cheese; oxen, for all the summer's work of cultivation, and the hauling wood and lumber from the forest to the home, and the ship-yard or the saw-mill. They also kept large flocks of hens and turkeys and ducks, — a supply for the home and the market. They thus lived an independent, simple, patriarchal life, every individual active, industrious, and busy. Before the building of the mills below my father's garden, the Major often went, as he told me, at the proper season, and, stationing himself on stones one on each side of the deepest passage in the river, secured, with a pitch-fork, many a shad, and sometimes a salmon.

Was this not a higher and more respectable life than many of the country people live now? For the females, especially, it was better and healthier than most of the forms of life that have succeeded to it in country towns. The large wheel obliged them to throw their arms out and backward, so as to open the chest fully and naturally, to walk backward and for-ward perfectly erect, so as to develop their muscles and give them the best and most graceful shape of which the female form is capable.

The Major had a son, Abner, living at home with him, when I came home from Dummer Academy. He had been on many voyages at sea; and when at home, was occupied with ship-building and boat-building, or with fishing along the coast. He invited me to go down the river with him, and out to sea, often to spend the night, teaching me the management of a boat, the throwing of the killick, the use of an oar and the rud-der, and showing me the best spots to fish for cod and haddock, bass and pollock, and entertaining me with stories of his sea life. A few hours commonly enabled us to fill our small boat, and then to sail or row back. I became much interested in this sport, and, when

2

Abner went to sea, took these little voyages with young men whom I knew. Before he went, I accompanied him, and once, as I was fishing, told Abner I believed my hook had become fastened to something at the bottom, for I could not move it. He took hold of my line, and immediately said, "You have hooked a halibut; now, keep your line free from the gunwale, or he will break it. Keep always firm hold, and pull carefully. When he refuses to come upward, let him go down. He will soon be tired, and will yield again." I kept hold, sometimes pulling up a few fathoms, and then letting him gradually go down. Changing, as Abner called it, with him for half an hour, I at last saw his head, and told Abner. "Steady!" said he, and stationed himself on my right with a gaff in his hands, and setting another man also with a gaff on my left. As I pulled the fish to within two feet or less of the surface, each of them struck in his gaff, just at or below the gills, and we drew him on board. I was naturally elated at my luck, or skill as I counted it. The fish was what seemed to me enormous; I have forgotten his dimensions, but only remember that, when weighed, his was found something more than twice my own weight.

The late season, October, brought the time for night fishing in deep water, for hake and cusk. For this we sailed down the river in the afternoon, furnished ourselves with clams or other suitable bait, and rowed or sailed to a point nine miles from the shore, the best known for night fishing. Here we took in sail, threw down our killick,— a wooden anchor weighted with stone, — took our supper, and put in our lines, twice as long as those for shallower waters. Our place was so well chosen that we always had luck, and often took in, by one or two o'clock in the morning, as many as our boat would safely hold. I then told my fellows to go to sleep in the bows, and I would watch in the stern sheets till morning. This we usually did, and my men slept till daybreak ; we then drew up our killick, hoisted sail. and made for the shore.

Once, when we had been very lucky and my men had turned in early, I found a fair wind just at daybreak, hoisted sail, took up killick, and steered for Mousum River, found water deep enough to enter the mouth, sailed up, and moored in the boat's place, and then waked my fellows, who were agreeably surprised to find themselves in port, at home.

We had a variety of adventures. Once, in a very dark night, I perceived by the sound that something was coming towards us. I ordered the men to take instantly to their oars, pulled vigorously upon the cable myself, and had the satisfaction of perceiving a large vessel pass directly over the place we had just occupied. There was no light on board, and nobody to hear our shouts.

We had several other pieces of luck which it pleased me more to tell of than my mother to listen to ; so that at last she absolutely refused to give her consent to my going on a night voyage. Before this, however, I had enjoyed a sight which I must describe. It was in that part of autumn when the sea, in our latitude, is phosphorescent. I had observed a little of it for several nights, but this night every ripple gave a flash of light. Our lines were visible for forty feet in the water, and the fishes we caught came up as masses of brilliant, golden light. We fished with two hooks to each line, and often brought up pairs of fine fishes. Once, each of us three was drawing up, at the same moment, two fishes; with them came the entire school, so that the whole ocean, to the depth of forty feet, was flashing with the most vivid light. All these fishes remained near the surface for ten minutes or more, when they began to descend, but were still visible, like thousands of flashes of lightning, and to the depth of eighty or one hundred feet. For the whole night every motion, every little ripple, every wavelet, was a soft flash of beautiful light.

CHAPTER III.

I ENTERED college in 1813, and, with Joseph H. Jones, whom I had met at Dummer Academy, had a room assigned us at 11 Massachusetts Hall, under Edward Everett, the tutor in Latin. Mr. Everett was very kind to me, and continued my friend to the end of his life.

The first visit I made, after being established in college, was to the Botanic Garden, to learn from Prof. Peck the names of the plants I had examined in Wells, for which I had found no names. He recognized them instantly from my description.

The first term in college was one of delightful study, varied by the pleasure of becoming acquainted with my classmates, some of whom became distinguished men, and two of them, George Bancroft and Caleb Cushing, represented our country at foreign courts; and several of whom, Rev. S. J. May, Hon. S. Salisbury, Hon. S. E. Sewall, have been my best and dearest friends through life.

At the end of the first term I went home, expecting to spend the vacation there; but on Saturday, the next day after my arrival, a man came from a school district five miles off, to engage my brother — some years older than myself — to teach the winter school in Maryland district. "You have come too late," said my father; "my son went off yesterday to Boston, to attend the medical lectures." "But who is this tall fellow? Why can't he come?" "He is a boy, only sixteen years old, who has come home from college to spend his vacation." It was, however, soon agreed that I should go and teach the school; and on Monday morning I went, in my father's sleigh, to Maryland Heights, where I taught, or rather very satisfactorily kept, a school of about twenty pupils, of both sexes, and all ages between four and twenty, for eight or nine weeks, the usual length of the term. I boarded with an old sea-captain, retired from service, whose maiden sister of forty years or more, unable to walk, had passed her time in carefully reading some of the best books in our language. Her favorites were Addison and Milton, about whose works she was always delighted to talk; and I have often recalled her observations upon striking passages in "Paradise Lost" as among the best and most delicate criticisms that have ever come to my knowledge. My boarding constantly with Captain Hatch was an experiment. Always before, the school-master had "boarded round," a week with each substantial householder in the district. A pleasant relic of this custom was that the school-master should sup with some one family, with each in turn, every week during the term. The supper was very good, — as good as the resources of the farms and forests and streams could furnish. It was always early, and was followed by dancing and games, frolic and fun, continued to a very late hour. It was sometimes eleven o'clock before I reached home at Captain Hatch's.

It was the fashion in those days for some good scholar to test the capacity of the teacher by offering some very difficult questions in arithmetic; and in the course of the first week, a very bright fellow, nineteen or twenty years old, was authorized to puzzle me. He brought a question which was really a very hard one, as merely an arithmetical question; but I had learned something of geometry, and this question depended upon a proposition of Euclid. I saw into it at once, and showed him not only how he might solve that question, but several others depending upon the same theorem. I was tried no more. On the contrary, I had a perfectly pleasant school from beginning to end, — not a harsh word nor a disrespectful look.

During the winter of the Sophomore year, I was not well enough to teach; but in the Junior year I was persuaded to supply the place of a much older man, in a school in Saco, ten miles from my father's. It was made up of the sons and daughters of saw-millers on Saco Falls, who kept the mills going, night and day. The girls were always well disposed, and gave me no trouble; but their brothers, taking after fathers who were almost always profane and unprincipled drunkards, were as impudent and stubborn as boys could be. I had, for the only time in my life, to depend upon the ferule and other implements of brute force. It was only when they found that I was fearless, and resolved, at any cost, to be master, that they submitted. It was with as great pleasure, for a moment, as I ever felt, that, sitting at breakfast one Monday morning, on my return from my father's, where I always spent Sunday, I was surprised by a sudden light, and looking back, saw from the window the ruinous old school-house in flames.

In the Senior year I kept, as many other fellow-collegians did, a school in the country for ten or twelve weeks. My school was at Bolton, and was superintended by the minister of the town, the excellent Father . Allen. The parents of nearly all the pupils were farmers, well-behaved and respectable people, whose children never gave me the least trouble, but made very surprising progress in all the branches then commonly taught in the country schools, — reading, spelling, arithmetic, and geography.

Several of my college friends taught in the same town, all of whom took respectable positions in after life; and we had some very pleasant evening meetings at Mr. Allen's, and in the houses of other hospitable gentlemen. By their frequent conversation with me, some of the young ladies acquired a taste for reading valuable books.

To this residence in Bolton I often look back with great pleasure. My boarding-house was very near the school, and at noon I always had half an hour to myself every day. Many of these half-hours I devoted to committing to memory lines in Greek, and always found I could learn, every day, thirty lines of the Iliad. I thus found that I had a good memory; I suppose that, if I had continued thus to exercise it daily, I might have retained it till now. But, for three years from that winter, the state of my eyes was such that I could not use them at all; and when those years were passed, I found my memory poor.

CHAPTER IV.

AFTER the spring vacation in 1814, I went back to college. Everything began as usual. One evening I returned from a pleasant visit to some newly made acquaintances, and was accosted by my room-mate, Joseph H. Jones, with whom I had been reading Lord Teignmouth's " Life of Sir William Jones," "Chum, Sir William says that to sleep more than four hours in one night is being an ox." " Well," said I, " I do not wish to be an ox, though I have a great respect for that animal. Shall we try the four-hour plan?" " Yes, and begin it this very evening." " But how about waking, after the four hours' sleep? " " To-morrow's prayer-bell will wake us at six. We may study till two o'clock every night; and to save our eyes somewhat, read alternately, aloud, for the last two hours, some pleasant book in English." I trusted in Jones, but I have no doubt he was mistaken, especially when I call to mind those genial and inspiring lines of Sir William : —

> " Six hours to law, to soothing slumber seven,
> Four to the world allot, and all to heaven."

So it was agreed. I sat down immediately to study Greek. The class had been reading the Anabasis. I liked it, and found it very easy, and instantly deter-

2

mined to read the whole of it. As I went on, it became easier and easier, and I found that the meaning in the lexicon, for a new word, was almost always very nearly what I had suspected on reading it. This happened so frequently that, before finishing the first volume, it occurred to me that I might read without the lexicon, just as the Greek boys must have done, long before lexicon or grammar was invented. This I did, having the lexicon by me, but using it only for such words as *parasang* (a measure of distance), or some entirely new word. I finished the Anabasis and the Cyropædia, and then the History of Greece, and some other works of Xenophon. I now felt confident I was pursuing the right course. We all read our English books in this way, and French and Italian when we have made a little progress. Nearly all the reading in the world must be without a dictionary.

When I was satisfied with Xenophon, I read Herodotus through in the same manner, and all that is to be found of Hesiod, and all I could find of Anacreon. I also read some Latin books, — the Letters of Pliny the Younger, and some of the charming philosophical works of Cicero. While doing this I never neglected my regular lessons, but learned them more thoroughly than ever; Jones did the same; so that we rose, in the opinion of our classmates and tutors, from a low to a respectably high place in the class.

We had pursued this course many weeks, agreeing to take at least half an hour's exercise in the pleasantest part of the day, and to be careful not to eat too much, when I was surprised by a pain in the left side. As I was a country doctor's son, and had often made blister-

ing plasters, and knew how to apply them and why, I
went to the apothecary's and got one to apply to my
own side. The relief was immediate, but not lasting.
A pain came next in my right side. Another blister
had only quite a temporary effect; so I applied another
to the middle of my chest. This had only the effect of
multiplying the pain, which now seized upon almost
every part of my body, and I felt myself seriously ill. I
went to the president to ask leave of absence. Dr.
Kirkland seemed always to know what was going on.
" So, Emerson," he said, in his paternal manner, " your
plan has not succeeded. I was afraid it would be so.
I am sorry. You are seriously ill, and had better go
home to your father as soon as possible."

My chum was affected as seriously, but very differ-
ently. His head was drawn down by a severe pain in
his neck, from which he never entirely recovered. He
was taken home to the house of a sister of one of our
classmates (Francis Jenks), and treated as kindly and
anxiously as if she had been his own sister.

I went immediately into Boston, and, at the end of
Long Wharf, went on board a coaster commanded by a
friend, who was soon to sail. I immediately went down
into the cabin, turned into a berth, and fell asleep.
Early in the night the sea became rough, and the toss-
ing of the vessel threw me into a most hideous dream.

We landed next morning at Kennebunk Harbor, from
which I soon found a conveyance to my father's house.
The kind old man, as soon as he understood my case,
began by congratulating me upon my escape. " Why
did you not tell me what experiment you were going to
make? I could have told you how it would end."

As soon as I was well enough, which was after not many days, I was mounted on an easy horse, one of my former friends, and kept riding almost every day for three months. I rode over all the good and pleasant roads and some of the bad ones, in almost every part of the county. I visited nearly all the towns ; rode by the oldest roads, those nearest the sea, on the marine border of Wells and York and Kittery, to Portsmouth. Thence across the Piscataqua to my grandfather's hospitable house in York. Thence to the top of Agamenticus, the highest hill in the county, commanding Portsmouth and all the hills and most of the towns in the county, and a noted landmark for sailors far out at sea. Thence to Berwick, where I had a delightful visit at a cousin's, and going thence, the next morning, saw abundant evidence, in the impassableness of the roads from the fall of many tall old trees, of the violence of the great gale of 1814.

Three months of such travelling, five or six hours every day in the week, in pleasant weather, in sunshine and pure air, through variegated and charming scenery, hills, rivers, the seaside, woods, old forests full of trees, and open cultivated plains, by farms and gardens, rendered me fit to return safely to my studies at college. Only one thing made me seriously regret having been absent from college. This was my failing to sympathize with my friend, S. J. May, in his success, new for a freshman, in getting the first prize for a dissertation. But this I did not learn till I saw him, on my return to Cambridge.

My father said it was now safe for me to go back, on condition that I would not aim at being a first-rate scholar, but that I should get my lessons faithfully, and spend much of my time in reading pleasant and amusing books. " Such as what, father?" " Don Quixote, and after that, anything else you can find equally good." So I went back under orders to read Don Quixote; which I did, but did not succeed in finding anything else equally good. An excellent substitute I found in Scott's novels, which I read with delight as they came out, and which I would recommend to others, even now, as better than almost anything that has come since. I confess that I have not read all nor one fifth part of the novels that have succeeded; I only speak of what I have read, which are those that have been most commended.

I enjoyed myself in college as much as any person could. The friendships I formed there have had the happiest effect upon my life, which would have been a very different and a much poorer thing without them. There are a thousand things which it would be pleasant to commemorate, but there is one only which I wish to dwell upon. Half a dozen good friends, lovers of study, agreed to spend together, at Cambridge, the vacation at the end of the Junior year, to study certain things we had had no opportunity to learn in the college course. We agreed to breakfast together, then to separate and pursue such occupations as we pleased till dinner-time; then to dine, and together go on with such studies as we pleased, and after tea to study the constellations, which we had had no opportunity to learn in college.

Caleb Cushing, now our minister in Spain, and myself agreed to spend our afternoons together in looking up the plants to be found in Cambridge. This we did very satisfactorily, and matured tastes which we have both since gratified.

We furnished ourselves with celestial globes and lamps, and studied night after night, until we knew all the constellations that were visible in the evening at that season of the year. No study I pursued in college has given me so much real satisfaction as this. I never see one of those constellations without experiencing a pleasure which no other object in nature gives me. I rejoice to know that in some of the best schools in Boston this study has already been introduced. Every person, tolerably well educated, should know the constellations.

Our Senior year was a pleasant one. I learned with ease all the lessons required, and thus had time for voluntary studies. I went on with my Greek, and read, in the course of the year, all of Homer except the last book of the Odyssey. In the winter vacation, at my boarding-house in Bolton, which was near the school, I repeatedly committed to memory thirty lines of Homer in thirty minutes. I mention this to record the shameful fact that, from neglecting fairly to use my memory for four or five years from that time, I lost it almost entirely, and it has ever since been a poor one. I have never known a person whose memory continued to be good, and even to improve in ripe age, who did not habitually exercise it, on poetry or something other than the poor affairs and business of daily life.

In the course of that Senior year I gradually forgot my father's caution, and took again too much to study, often continued till late at night, until I waked one morning with pain in my eyes, which I soon found would make it impossible to read more than an hour or two a day. My only consolation was that it gave me time to mature my acquaintance with my college friends : for ˙the most important of the many advantages of a college education is the opportunity of becoming well acquainted with persons of one's own age, and of forming intimacies with the best and most congenial. Many of my very best friends have been my classmates, with several of whom I continued intimate as long as they lived ; and now two of the very dearest friends I have are friends of more than sixty years. ·

CHAPTER V.

I GRADUATED at Harvard College in 1817, and went, immediately after my recovery from an illness which almost overpowered me on Commencement day, home to my father's in Wells. I had lived economically, but was indebted for about one-fourth part of my college expenses, so that I felt somewhat anxious. My father had always had extensive practice, but it was among families most of whom were poor. My brother and I often urged him, when we were posting up his accounts, to send bills to those who were most and had been longest in debt to him. But he always made answer, "They are poor; when they can afford it they will pay. Meanwhile they will bring us wood and hay, and other products of their farm or their fishing."

I had been at home two days when a letter came from Dr. Kirkland, offering me the place of master in an excellent private school in Lancaster, established by several most respectable men, with a salary of $500 a year. This was then a large salary, and I thankfully accepted the offer, which relieved me from all anxiety.

I went immediately to Cambridge to see Dr. Kirkland, and from him to Bolton, to Mr. Stephen Higginson, and to Lancaster to Rev. Dr. Thayer, who became, and always continued, my excellent friends.

The school had been limited to twenty-five pupils, who paid, each, five dollars a quarter. I had not been at work more than five or six weeks before the discovery was made, or was thought to be made, that I had uncommon skill as a teacher and as a manager of boys, and men came from the neighboring towns begging that their boys might be admitted, so that, before the end of the second quarter, there were forty-two pupils, as many as the house could hold. The conductors of the school, in their generosity, saw fit to increase the price of tuition twenty-five per cent, so that my pay was more than twice as much as they had offered, and my indebtedness soon ceased.

My eyes were so poor that I could not look into a Greek book or a Latin; but my knowledge of both languages was such that this was not necessary, and I had only to make the boys read distinctly, and loud enough for me to hear with ease. The discipline in my school, though such as was common in those days, was bad in every respect. I kept a switch and a ferule, and used them both, often feeling, as I did so, like a malignant spirit, and sometimes acting in an evil spirit. I have many times wished that I could ask the pardon of one boy whom I had punished unjustly and in passion. But he never came to see me, and I have no doubt he retained, perhaps always, a righteous grudge against me. I had a head to every class, and urged my boys to strive to reach and to retain it, by medals and commendation, — medals for daily ornament, and medals for permanent holding. So far as I knew, nobody objected to the punishments or to the rewards. I had, occasionally, my own scruples and doubts in regard to

both. It is a melancholy fact that, notwithstanding
these objections, my school was.considered as, on the
whole, very kindly and well managed. I certainly was
reasonable and kind toward all my good boys, and the
two youngest of them all, whom I now meet every week,
have always been and are among my best and kindest
friends.

Many of my boys were from Boston, and boarded in
families where no control over them was even attempted. I saw the evil of this state of things, and
wrote to the parents, proposing, if I should be sustained, to hire a large house, and get a respectable
family, and take all the boys with me to it, so that I
might have them all near me, and maintain a constant oversight of them. This plan was approved and
carried into execution, to the manifest benefit of some
of the boys. I rejoiced, and was thus rewarded for the
increased care. But I gradually, without suspecting
why, lost my vigorous health and my spirits, which I
endeavored to retain by buying a horse and riding every
day before breakfast. The country is very variegated
and pleasant, with hills and forests and little lakes, and
the beautiful Nashua winding among the cultivated
fields and Wachuset rising up behind them in the west,
so that riding was very pleasant. The elms and hickories of Lancaster are finer, I have always been inclined
to think, than those I have seen in any other part of
Massachusetts; the native willows on the banks of the
Nashua are larger than I have found elsewhere, and
the sugar-maples along some of the roads are not less
promising and beautiful.

I had, to sustain me, many very kind friends. I can

never forget the wise and paternal advice and care of
Dr. Thayer, the never-failing kindness of all the family
of Mr. Higginson, and the almost motherly affection of
Mrs. R. J. Cleveland, who, with her sisters, lived very
near my school, so that I could and did visit them at
all hours of the day and evening. This generous
friendship lasted to the end of the lives of Mrs. Cleveland and her husband, and so far, through the lives of
their children, and has been a blessing to me always.
I accepted every invitation from the kind people of
Lancaster, and enjoyed their little parties, especially
dancing, of which I was very fond; and once I rode,
for that enjoyment, to Leominster, danced all the evening, and came home at an early hour next morning.

I continued, for two years, successful and prosperous,
so as to be able to begin the education, in my own
school, of my two younger brothers. My daily exercise
on horseback sustained me, but could not make me well,
so that I was continually growing weaker and sadder.
At the beginning of a vacation, after I had sent all the
boys home, I mounted my horse, one Monday morning,
with a feeling that I might possibly reach home by
the end of the week, and so spend my last days with
my parents. I trotted slowly along, but turned round
on a hill in Harvard and bade a last, silent farewell to
Lancaster, so much endeared to me, and then slowly
pursued my journey, hoping to reach Groton and spend
the night. I did reach it before dinner-time, feeling
better than I had for months, with my anxieties all
nearly gone. I stopped at a comfortable inn, had my
horse cared for, took a good dinner and a comfortable
nap, and awoke fresh, hopeful, and surprisingly strong, ◄

so that I presently resolved to go on. I grew stronger every hour, and I was able to reach home in three days, instead of six, feeling and looking so well that no one suspected me of having been otherwise.

I continued my pleasant work at Lancaster for two years, at the end of which I received a letter from President Kirkland, inviting me to become a tutor in the Mathematical Department in Harvard College. At the same time a letter came from the President to Dr. Thayer, informing him that a senior, Solomon P. Miles, whom he could recommend highly in every respect, might be persuaded to take my place. The arrangement was easily made : Mr. Miles came to Lancaster, I bade farewell to my good friends there, and rode on my own horse to Cambridge. 1 had become fond of the animal, and had my pocket full of money, — was richer, indeed, in feeling, than I have ever been since.

All the time I was at Lancaster, I daily regretted the sad state of my eyes, and submitted, in vain, to all kinds of remedies. I was unable to read, which I should have done every night for three or four hours. If I had been able to do so, the additional labor would undoubtedly have quite destroyed my health ; so that the apparent affliction was really my salvation. Besides, the apparent loss in book-learning was more than compensated by the knowledge gained of human character, in its highest and best as well as its ordinary forms.

CHAPTER VI.

MY residence at Cambridge was very pleasant. President-Kirkland was one of the kindest, most agreeable, and benignant persons in the world. Professor Farrar, head of the Mathematical Department, had all the qualities which command the respect and affection of students, so that he was a universal favorite. He was always very kind to me, and we took many pleasant rides together. Professor Frisbie, professor of Latin, was a most amiable man of great sense and deep thought, and an excellent scholar. His eyes were so poor that he could not use them, and he commonly sat in the recitation-room with a handkerchief drawn over them. He seldom interrupted a poor scholar, except for some egregious blunder; but while a good scholar was translating, and failed to give the best word, he threw it to him instantly. One of the best Latin scholars, a tutor in Latin when I was there, and afterwards professor, told me that these interjected words did him more good than any other instruction he ever received.

Dr. Hedge, professor of logic and metaphysics, was a kindly, pleasant gentleman. The elder Rev. Dr. Henry Ware was a sort of grandfather to all of us younger teachers, and to all most pleasant and genial.

Mr. Caleb Cushing came soon to join us, as tutor in mathematics; and not long after, Edward Everett came, as professor of the Greek language and literature, and George Ticknor, as lecturer on French literature. These were all most agreeable gentlemen to be associated with. Rev. Mr. Norton, who had been librarian, was professor in the Theological School. His eyes were, like mine, such as not to allow him the use of books by night, and I called at his room one evening, hoping not to find myself an intruder. He received me most graciously, and invited me to come again, and often. He was one of the best thinkers I have ever known, and although he spoke very slowly in conversation, I often left him with a feeling that I had learned more than I ever learned in the same space of time from any other person. I still considered myself a teacher, and, guided by his opinion, I read, as far as my eyes would permit, everything that was desirable for a person seeking to find out how to teach well. I read with admiration Milton's tractate on "the reforming of education, one of the greatest and noblest designs that can be thought on, and for want thereof, this nation perishes," — our own as well as Milton's; and I got some real instruction from Roger Ascham, gathered, like wheat, from a large mass of chaff.

The serious, religious conversation of Mr. Norton led me gradually to compare the course I had pursued as a teacher with the course which, as a Christian teacher, I ought to have pursued. On thinking upon the subject, I more and more confidently came to the conclusion that exciting the emulation of children was heathenish, respectable in Cicero, but not to be tolerated in one who accepted the doctrine of Paul, — " in honor preferring one another " ; that inflicting cruel bodily pain on a child was savage and almost brutal ; and that, if I ever again should have the management of boys confided to me, I should avoid both.

I enjoyed hearing, occasionally, Edward Everett's most eloquent lectures and his charming conversation. My own engagements, as a teacher, prevented my hearing Mr. 'licknor's lectures except very rarely. He sometimes called at my room when he had, driving from Boston, reached Cambridge early, and he often called there after his lecture, and met students in law, and other residents who were attracted by his reputation and by his courteous manners and instructive and agreeable conversation. I became somewhat intimate with him, went often to his father's house in Boston, and thus formed an acquaintance which was one of the blessings of my life, as it continued to the end of his. Every one may now learn how valuable such a friendship was by reading his " Life, Letters, and Journals," which have just issued from the press, and which give life-like pictures of a greater number of distinguished persons in this country, and in many parts of Europe, than any book which has been published in our time. With Mr. Edward Everett I became much more intimate. He and Mr. Cushing and myself were much younger than the other members of the college government, and often went out to walk and exercise together. The house he occupied had a large garden, surrounded by a wall high enough to protect those within from the students' eyes ; and we often went there at noon to take exercise which we did not wish to exhibit. Within the garden was an unoccupied barn, which served as a place of refuge in rainy weather. I have still several notes of that time from Mr. Everett, which say only, " On saute à midi."

During this period I was tutor in mathematics and natural philosophy. I was very fond of both, and as I had studied them well in college, I found no necessity of much preparation for hearing lessons in them. As to teaching, I attempted nothing of the kind, except that I sometimes drew figures on the wall, to point out an application. In the department, much most excellent teaching was given by Professor Farrar, whose lectures on natural philosophy and astronomy I have never known surpassed or equalled. I have seen, day after day, a whole class so charmed by one of his lectures as to forget the approach of the Commons hour, and to leave, with reluctance, to go to dinner, though the lecture had gone more than half an hour beyond the time allotted to it. When, some years later, an attempt was made to change the course of things, in consequence of the want of teaching in the college, Mr. Farrar alone said he did not see the necessity of a change ; and so far as his own department was concerned, there was no necessity. He gave as much of actual teaching as is often given, even now, in any department in any college. If the same had been done in every department, little change could have been thought necessary.

One of the greatest advantages of my residence in Cambridge was the kindness I received from Dr. N. Bowditch, the great American mathematician. He was a member of the corporation, and, seeing the interest

I took in teaching, or rather hearing lessons, in that department, he invited me to come and see him at Salem. I gladly accepted the invitation, and enjoyed, very greatly, more than one visit. He perceived the difficulties I had with my eyes, and once told me that, at about my age, he had suffered in the same way, trying doctors and their prescriptions in vain ; but it occurred to him that the eye was made for the light, and light for the eye, and that, when he went out, he ought to take the sunniest side of the street, and not the shady side ; and that the irritation in his eyes might be allayed by the application of cold water. He tried that, opening his eyes in cold water, first in the morning and last at night, and whenever they seemed to need it, and continuing the act till the irritation was gone. In a few weeks his eyes were well, and had so continued all his life. I tried the experiments, in every particular, and in a few weeks my eyes were perfectly well, and have so continued up to this day. They would not bear, however, the looking into blazes or red-hot bottles or crucibles, and I was obliged to forego the advantage I hoped to gain, in the study of chemistry, by going every day into the laboratory of Dr. Gorham, who was then giving lectures on that science.

I was very much interested in mathematics, and when it became necessary for Professor Farrar to go to the Azores, on account of the health of his wife, I undertook to go on with the translation of a French work on the Calculus, and get it ready for the press. This I did, and had it printed, with my introduction and notes, so that, when Mr. Farrar returned, he found it ready for use of the college. He was agreeably surprised

3

and highly gratified, and almost immediately urged me
to remain in college, and become professor in mathematics. " The work I have to do in astronomy and
natural philosophy," he said, " is enough for one person, and I delight in them, and shall be glad to continue to teach them ; but I do not like nor understand
mathematics as you do. This department will necessarily be divided very soon : why not consent to stay
here as professor of mathematics ? " I was naturally
much gratified, but was not prepared to embrace his
offer, although very kindly seconded by President
Kirkland.

I enjoyed my life at college very heartily. There
was always a meeting, every Sunday evening, at the
president's, at which Dr. Popkin, Mr. Brazer, tutor,
and afterwards professor of Latin, and some others
were sometimes present ; and always Mr. Everett, Mr.
Cushing, and myself. Mr. Farrar and his wife, who
had been Miss Buckminster, kept the president's house,
and were always present when she was well ; usually a
niece of the president, and, almost always, Mrs. Farrar's
three sisters. These were far the most pleasant and
really the most brilliant parties I have ever attended.
Mr. Everett was always full of fun and pleasant stories
and anecdotes ; Mr. Cushing often gave a foretaste
of the brilliant powers which he afterward exhibited in
other scenes ; and the pre-eminent talents of the Buck-
minsters gracefully showed themselves in their natural
light. We young people usually grouped ourselves in
a corner round Mr. Everett, who always, when he saw
the door of the study open, stilled us instantly with,
" Hush now ! the president is coming."

It was not pleasant to think of quitting these occupations and scenes, but as often as I reflected, after an
evening with Mr. Norton, on what ought to be the government and teaching of a school, among Christians, I
felt inclined, and at last resolved, that if an opportunity
should offer, I would myself try what could be done by
one possessed of this idea. Such an opportuuity soon
presented itself. Looking over the *Sentinel*, I found an
advertisement to this effect : " Whoever wishes to be a
candidate for the place of master of the English Classical School, about to be established, will apply to the
committee," — giving the names of some of the individuals.

In the autumn vacation of 1820 a party of us proposed to visit the White Mountains, in New Hampshire.
This party consisted of Wm Ware, of the class of 1816,
and J. Coolidge, C. Cushing, S. J. May, S. E. Sewall,
and myself, of 1817. We were to meet in Kennebunk,
at my father's, and thence proceed, on such horses and
in such conveyances as could be procured, to the mountains.

We accordingly met there, and on the very next
morning, accompanied by J. E. Moody, set off, and
travelled through Limeric, Waterboro', Broomfield, El-
lenwood Bend, Parsonsfield, to Mrs. McMillan's, at
Conway.

Our road still lay along the river, which was always
to be heard dashing in foam over the rocks that form its
bed. The hills sometimes receded, leaving rich green
intervales, which were here and there cultivated, and
sometimes adorned with a peasant's cottage. At other
places the hills approached the stream, and left only

space for a narrow road by its side. At one place the way had been entirely formed along the base of cliff that had projected into the river, and which still hung beetling over the traveller as he passed.

It was nearly dark when we arrived at the house of Crawford, the guide to the mountains. We found that our companions had reached this house soon enough to avoid most of the rain, by which we had found ourselves completely drenched. In the evening, seated round a large fire, we made our arrangements to ascend, if the weather should permit, the mountains to-morrow. Mrs. Crawford was busily employed in cooking provisions, and we not less busily in hoping for fair weather. The morning of Thursday proved fair, and, as our guide could not get ready till late in the forenoon, the individuals of our party were engaged in amusing themselves as the taste of each inclined. Some of us climbed the neighboring hills, some went to shoot pigeons, others strolled along the river, and nearly all, at one time or other, endeavored to sketch some of the grand and novel views this place presented.

Towards noon preparations were ended, and we set off for the Notch. Several of. us were mounted on horseback, and the other, with our guide, drove on in a wagon. We were hemmed in by mountains whose ridges extended parallel to the river, here and there divided or receding, to admit the tributary streams. They usually rose precipitously from the banks, and seemed to present, as we advanced, continually more and more grand and interesting scenery. Sometimes the mountains retired to a distance from each other, and the river, which usually dashed with tumult and impetuosity over a rocky bed, meandered more gently and silently through the intervale, and the tall trees which grew on its banks bent over the road, excluding every distant object, and presented, by the deep gloom they produced, a strong contrast to the light and elevation of all we had just been viewing.

It seemed a calm, delightful retirement, as would a sequestered scene of domestic life to one who had been long toiling in the rough and cheerless paths of business or ambition. After wending awhile through this still, twilight woods, and allowing us to enjoy its shade and seclusion, the road brought us again into the midst of views of rocks and mountains ; and as we emerged from the thicket the beauty of each object seemed to be increased, and the effects of distance and grandeur heightened by their having been for a time concealed from our view. We were particularly struck with the ruggedness of a long, high hill which towered up on our right.

Between the road and its base roared the Saco. Its side was composed of large round stones, piled so loosely on each other that it seemed as if a footstep would have displaced and precipitated them into the river and plain below. Above, all was lonely and bare, save that the summit was crowned with a few scathed old trees, which distance diminished to the size of a schoolboy's staff. Toward the upper end of this valley a solitary house looked out upon the bleakest and most desolate spot that peasant ever chose for his habitation. This was the last house, and here we were obliged to leave our horses, and travel the rest of the way on foot. The road was rough and ascending, but the rocks and torrents too much interested our attention to suffer us to think of or feel its wearisomeness.

The mountains on each hand approached nearer, and became more precipitous; and far above us were seen the torrents glancing in the sun as they dashed impetuously down the ravines or were poured over the rocks in their way to join the river. The river now dwindled to a brawling, shallow brook, which still has scarcely room for its passage, and even this is shared by the road, built on stones against the very side of a high and threatening precipice. This place is called the Notch, and seems to have been made by some convulsion which rent the mountain and opened the passage for the waters of what was once a lake. From this place the road in each direction descends, and the mountains on every side rise.

Here we were to leave the road, and here we rested and took some refreshment. As we were now to plunge into the woods, we arranged our baggage so as to be as little incommoded by it as possible. Each person was furnished with a blanket, and several of us had cloaks, against the night encampment on the mountain. These we made into a bundle and fastened on our shoulders, so as to have our arms at liberty. The guide carried the provisions, fire apparatus, and an axe, and I had a fowling-piece, to shoot at the game that might present itself; it was thought best that I should go first with the gun in my hand, powder and shot slung under my arm, and a snug pack on my shoulders, so I led the way two or three rods in advance. We struck off directly into the thick woods, guided by the course of a brook that dashed down among the tall trees from one side of the hill. This we crossed, clambered up the rugged opposing bank, over the trunks of windfall trees, and soon found ourselves in a rude path, which the guide had formed some weeks before by removing many of the fallen trees and cutting away some of the growing ones. The way was still, however, rugged and difficult enough, always ascending, sometimes winding about a ledge of rocks or clump of trees, too perpendicular or too close to be passed over or penetrated, and sometimes leading us straight up a steep side, now compelling us to make a cautious and uncertain footing among the rocks, and now to mount over the prostrate trunks which had been left to serve as a ladder. As we ascended, the trees gradually diminished in size and height. The elms, oaks, and maples successively disappeared, and no others were to be seen but evergreens, with here and there a stunted poplar or birch.

Our spirits were fresh and high, and we were animated with the aspiring and impatient feeling of young men and adventurers, but we were repeatedly obliged to stop and rest, before we reached our proposed place of encampment. This was a small plain among the woods, two thirds of the distance through the region of trees. Here we found a hut made like a hunter's lodge, previously built by the guide. It was formed by extending a pole, ten or twelve feet long, horizontally from one tree to another, at the height of about six feet from the ground, from which inclined several others, with one end resting on the ground. On these were spread long pieces of hemlock-bark covered with branches of fir in the fashion of tiles, forming a very close covering. As we were in each other's way, and there were still some hours before dark, and the first round top, as the guide told us, was at less than a mile's distance, three of us, Coolidge, Sewall, and myself, se' out to visit it. We were now relieved of our baggage, and of the guide and our tardy companions. This, our expedition, was undertaken from pure curiosity and love of exertion, and each of us valued himself on his activity. I enjoyed a singular advantage from my early habits of climbing hills and roaming the woods, and my companions were not men lightly to confess themselves outdone.

A distich* from one of Scott's poems, which all the scenery about had called up, and which burst at once from two of us, awakened the burning emulation of the clansman, which every young spirit has felt, and we darted forward through the woods and up the side of the mountain. It was still steeper than before, but we were not in a mood to yield to fatigue, and stopped not till we found ourselves meeting the perpendicular side of a rock overgrown with shrubs. Up this we soon scrambled, and sprang out upon a scene stranger and more wonderful than we had ever beheld or dreamed of before. It seemed as if that rock had lifted us into a new and vaster creation. The ground under our feet was covered with plants new and unknown, such as are found only on the tops of mountains or in the inhospitable regions of the north ; and on all sides were the mountains, piled in rude and grand magnificence we had formed no conception of. Beyond us, at a distance, towered a proud, gray, naked peak which could not be

---

* "Stung by such thoughts o'er bank and brae,
Like fire from steel, he glanced away."

mistaken. About its sides rested a thousand hills, with their bare rocks and immense forests slumbering, it seemed, in the mighty solitude and unbroken stillness of the birthday of creation. Nothing moved, but the thunder-clouds were mustering for a storm in the west, and the chill air admonished that night was already settling in the valleys. We returned with headlong rapidity, and found ourselves almost immediately at the encampment. As we were to stretch ourselves for the night on the floor of the lodge, we took care to strew it with fresh branches of fir, so arranged as to allow only the tops to be seen, and forming a dry and elastic bed. After having made a large fire directly before our hut, we took food, and, wrapped in our cloaks or blankets, stretched ourselves on the rustic bed for the night, and slept till the guide roused us to pursue our way.

We were enveloped in a thick and chilly fog, but, as the guide assured us it was no uncommon thing at that hour and that place, we had soon buckled on our bundles and were on the march. It seemed a wearisome length before we came to the same airy point to which some of us had before ascended ; and now the fog made it impossible to see a rod's distance, so that our elevation only gave the cold and searching northwest wind, loaded as it was with mist, a fairer and more exposed object. We passed over the top of one round hill, and then descended into the hollow which separated it from the next, and which was covered with thick evergreens three or four feet high, and throwing out long and tough horizontal limbs, so firm as often to allow one to walk over their tops, and so thickly interwoven as to

present an almost insurmountable obstacle to passing
between them. Then another hill-top and another belt
of dwarf firs. If, as the Indians used to think, a de-
mon still possessed this dreary region, jealous of any
inroads on his dominion, and who, besides stretching
about him the deep and dark forests, at the foot, and
above them the almost impenetrable barrier of stunted
evergreens, was ready to arm the elements against the
hardy wretch who should invade his consecrated realm,
he had now almost effected his purpose; for, weary
of the toilsome march, penetrated to the skin by the
fog, and shivering with cold from the raw mountain
air, without any hope of seeing the sun or of being
rewarded for the labors we had already undergone, as
it was impossible to see two rods before us, we were
almost tempted to turn back.   Added to this, our guide
discovered that he had lost his way.

After finding our way back to the right path, we
stopped in one of the hollows between the hills, under
the wretched covert of the dwarf trees, and, with much
difficulty, succeeded in kindling a fire and partially dry-
ing ourselves. But there was nothing like comfort to
be found here; several suffered exceedingly from the
cold. When we had been waiting two hours, and it
was nine o'clock, the sun suddenly burst out upon us,
and we immediately were on our way again. We now
went on with the greatest alacrity; and it was not long
before, having passed over several lower elevations, we
found ourselves on the top of the high and beautiful
round eminence which is called Mount Pleasant. The
name is well deserved. It is just so high as to lift its
top above the circle of vegetation, while it affords a

distant prospect of several cultivated valleys lying about their own streams. To the south is seen the spot occupied by the guide's house, which, though not less than nine or ten miles distant, in a line, is distinct; and beyond it are seen the scattered hamlets on the banks of the Saco. Far to the west can be descried the farms and houses on Amonoosuck, in Breton Wood; and farther still, the settlements in Jefferson.

In full view before us stood the object of our toil, the grand and solitary Mount Washington. At the bottom of the rocky vale between sparkled a little pond in its basin of rock, surrounded on three sides by hills, and on the fourth sending out a little rill, which is one source of the Amonoosuck. We waited on Mount Pleasant until our party had all come up and rested themselves; and then ran down the steep side, and were soon seated on the brink of the Punch-Bowl, as this little pond is called.

A short but toilsome part of our labor remained: it was to cross the low hill between us and the foot of the mountain, and climb to its summit over the loose, bare stones. From the brink of the little lake, the ascent seemed easy and gentle, and as if a few short steps would bring us without labor to the top, but long, thick moss covered and concealed the form of the rocks of the little hill, and rendered our footing extremely uncertain; so that many were the falls and bruises received before we reached the foot of Mount Washington, and often did we have to stop to rest ourselves in our perilous path up the steep and sharp rocks, piled, as they were, loosely on each other; for the torrents have carried away all the soil, and left the large stones entirely bare. Here and there, indeed, in the deep crevices, a little earth is left, and, in some places on the south side, protected by high rocks from the cutting gales, there are nooks where the sun rests, and beautiful flowers are seen springing up, and butterflies fluttering round them, and all looks and feels like summer. But mount the next crag, and the wind comes on you so cold, and the barrenness and desolation that meet you are so entire, that you can hardly persuade yourself that it is not winter.

From the top, what a grand view! Yet, the greatness comes on you by such slow degrees, that all the effect of surprise is lost, and there remains only that solemn, silent thoughtfulness and admiration which are entirely removed from the warmth and fervor of mind which a sudden and unexpected grandeur produces. All here is magnificent indeed, but all is savage and wild and desolate, as it was left by the hand of its Creator. Nothing at first strikes the eye but the bald, rocky peaks of mountains rising at intervals round the summit you stand on, and bared by the tempest of a thousand winters, and eternally preserving a wintry barrenness. A little lower, you see the tops of other hills, rough with the trunks of blasted trees ; and about and below all, the dark woods, deepening into a broad and monotonous ocean, broken only by the distant and unfrequent light reflected upwards from the surface of some solitary lake, or by the mountains that rise like islands amidst it. Nothing can exceed the sense of utter dreariness which takes possession of you when, throughout this boundless scene, you perceive not a vestige of the labor of man.

Though it was one o'clock, and a bright sun, we found the north side of the rock crusted with ice. It was bitterly cold, and the sharp northwest wind so chilled us as almost to deprive us of the use of our hands. We had no desire to remain in this place long, for the cold rendered it excessively uncomfortable, and the prospect was such as one need not desire long to dwell on. Entirely unlike anything I had ever seen, and made up of a few great features, it made such an impression that the picture, in all its bold outlines, is still, after more than fifty years, before me. The descent was almost without fatigue, though not without danger. To proceed rapidly it is necessary to spring down from rock to rock, and the impetus gained is such as to make it almost impossible sometimes to avoid the sharp rocks and precipices that suddenly present themselves. But reaching the foot, and passing along the west side of the little hill, we arrived safely on the borders of the pond.

Mount Pleasant was directly in our way, but the side towards us was exceedingly steep, and though we found no difficulty in descending, we were unanimous in thinking that we had had enough of climbing, for that day at least. So the guide undertook to lead us round the east side of the hill by a way which he knew, he said, but had not often travelled. This way we took, though it would be bold to say that we kept it, for we had to make a path for ourselves, leaping across deep clefts and over sloughs, and breaking through those tangled thickets just up to our shoulders, neither to be leaped over nor crept under, and climb along the side of precipices, holding on by the branches or roots of the struggling firs and birches, — places where there was not

the least sign that mortal had ever been before; and
ever and anon we crossed the rich purple beds of
cranberries and cornel berries, so temptingly luxuriant
that some of the weaker brethren could not resist,
but would linger behind till the guide and his companions were out of sight, and so take a wrong path
and get tangled in the thicket or suspended over a
gully. Finally, however, but not without many difficulties and more complaints, we got round Mount
Pleasant.

We now began to get among the lower and pleasanter
hills. For these have their tops covered with the alpine
plants which I mentioned, — objects of great curiosity to
us, admirers, as we professed to be, of the vegetable
world, and one at least a scientific observer. Many
of these were entirely new to us, and so different from
the usual plants of the temperate climate that we
have seldom had an entertainment of the kind more
agreeable.

Proceeding along a ridge of variable height, we occasionally caught a glimpse of scenes of peculiar beauty
when the hills allowed us to look down on a cultivated
spot by the borders of a lake or river, almost enveloped, as they always were, by the dark woods, and
always seeming to be in the centre of an amphitheatre
of mountains. Stopping sometimes to gaze on such
scenes, and stepping aside where we listed to indulge
any idle curiosity, and resting ourselves when and
where we chose, it was not long before we reached the
last green top, the same which I had visited the evening before. Here we stopped again for all to come up.

From the last round top there is a continual descent

through the woods to the Notch. It was but a short
distance to our last night's encampment, and there
three of our number, not caring to add to their fatigue,
determined to remain for the ensuing night. Leaving
the guide to keep up the fire and take charge of our
wearied companions, four of us, Cushing, Sewall,
Ware, and myself, resolved to go on to the Notch.
The sun, even where we were, far up on the mountain,
was scarcely half an hour high, and, in the valley, had
already been some time set, and the path we had.to
travel was steep, crooked, narrow, and often obstructed
by logs and rocks. We had no time to lose; waiting
but a moment, then, to arrange matters with our companions, we set off at a good travelling pace down the
hill. But we soon saw this would not do; the darkness at every step was evidently fast increasing. Our
only alternative, then, was to proceed at a much brisker
rate, or run the risk of spending the night on some
bank or under some rock in the woods. Putting myself again foremost, to avoid any danger from my fowling-piece, we pressed forward with such rapidity as the
road would admit. At first we sprang onward at a great
rate with perfect safety; but darkness gathered round
us so fast that it soon became difficult to discern the
path; and often did I leap forward entirely uncertain
what was before me, and only taking what seemed the
path's most probable direction. I was usually fortunate, but three times I went headlong over logs or
down slippery banks, and gained nothing by my falls
but the pleasure or the power of warning my companions to avoid them; and indeed they almost always
did avoid them, taking care to venture a leap only

when they saw I came off safely. Thus we contrived to keep the path until we crossed the brook within a few rods of the road. Here it was too dark to distinguish any traces of the way, but guiding ourselves by the noise of the brook, we soon emerged from the woods, not far from the place where we had entered them. We were only thirty-five minutes in accomplishing, in the twilight and dark, a descent which, by broad daylight, usually takes more than an hour. And right glad were we to see again the broad heavens and a plain road.

We had still two miles and a half to walk to the house where we expected supper. We had the whole evening, and a fine one, too, to walk this distance, and felt, moreover, no such disposition for active bodily exertion as would allow us to be very scrupulous about a few minutes more or less which it might take up. There was, indeed, when it occurred to us how sparsely we had dined, and the generous allowance of exercise we had since indulged in, a secret monition that something like a supper might at no distant time be far from unacceptable. Such thoughts, however, soon gave place to others more befitting the scene and the hour. We had reached the Notch. The towering cliffs on each side, garnished here and there by their own fir-trees, rested in bold relief on the starlit sky; behind us, in the western heavens, still glimmered that faint blush of soft light which, whether the last rays of departing day or a gleam from the northern aurora, served to relieve the deep gloom of the dark valley before us, and into which we were entering; while the dash of the Saco from below us on our left, as it fell over rocks, or chafed angrily against its precipitous banks, came up and mingled and harmonized with the whole.

As we walked slowly down this romantic valley we were frequently struck with a sparkle of light from among the rocks and woods, high up the mountain on our left. It appeared to be caused by the reflection of a bright planet from the smooth surface of some rock polished and moistened by the water which trickled over it, and looked like a star on the face of the mountain. Some such appearance as this probably gave rise to a tradition among the Indians, that somewhere on these mountains was a shining carbuncle, which hung very high over a lake, and was guarded by an immense and hideous serpent, one of the same race, doubtless, which from time immemorial has had charge of all inestimable treasures.

When we arrived at the lone house we were all most completely fatigued. We called for coffee and food of any kind, and comfortable beds as soon as they could possibly be made ready. The good woman seemed to have a feeling of true sympathy for us. Whatever it was, she set herself about the business with the readiest alacrity, and by dint of the most admirable management, in bestirring herself and moving others, succeeded beyond our fondest expectations. He who remembers the day of his life when he was most hungry and at the same time most fatigued, may have some faint conception of the deliciousness of our supper, the unutterable comfort of our repose.

On the morrow, without waiting for the remainder of our companions, we mounted our horses and returned

4

to the guide's house, through that wild valley which is
so beautiful that it is strange that all in New England
who can afford it, and who admire scenery, should not
go and visit it, and pass through the Notch at least,
and the young and vigorous ascend to the summit of
the mountain.

CHAPTER VII.

THE plan of a school, to be called the English Classical School, was adopted by the school committee of the town of Boston, June 20, 1820, on the report of a subcommittee, of which A. A. Wells, Esq., was chairman. At a town-meeting, Jan. 15, 1821, the plan was approved, only three in the negative. At a meeting of the school committee held Feb. 19, 1821, G. B. Emerson was unanimously chosen principal, but final action was deferred till a meeting held March 26, when the appointment was confirmed, and A. A. Wells, Rev. Charles Lowell, Rev. John Pierpont, Lemuel Shaw, Esq., and Benjamin Russell were chosen a committee on the English Classical School. —*Dr. Gould on the Schools of Boston.*

Having determined to be a candidate for the place of master of the English Classical School in Boston, I sought to get the expression from respectable persons of their belief in my competency to fulfil the duties of that place. President Kirkland and all the college professors gave me their names. The parents of many of my pupils at Lancaster kindly stated their favorable opinion, which was confirmed by good friends in Boston.

I sent in my application, and very soon received from one of the committee the statement that I had been unanimously chosen.

Mr. S. P. Miles accepted the invitation of Dr. Kirkland to take my place in college, and as soon as I could

I moved to Boston, and found a temporary home in a boarding-house.

To my great satisfaction I found that an old friend of mine, Mr. Lemuel Shaw, afterwards chief justice, was on the committee, and I went to him to ascertain whether I should be allowed to teach and manage the school according to my own ideas. He approved of them entirely, and said that, if I would make a short statement in writing of the course I wished to pursue, he would lay it before the committee, and he had little doubt that it would be approved. This I did, and, on my next visit, he told me that the committee had passed a vote that, as I had been chosen unanimously, as a person fully competent to fill the place, I should be allowed to manage it, in matters of instruction and discipline, according to my own views.

Official notice in the newspapers soon brought together in the Latin School-house, on School Street, all the boys who were desirous of admission to the English Classical. An intimation from the committee that a leading object in the establishment of this school was to raise the standard in the grammar schools, rendered it my duty to make the examination pretty thorough. Accordingly I carefully examined, in small divisions, for six hours every day for two weeks, the one hundred and thirty-five boys who presented themselves, of whom I judged seventy-five to be admissible.

The lower story of a school-house on Derne Street, on the spot now covered by the Reservoir, was prepared for the English Classical School, and on a Monday morning the seventy-five boys were present. I spent half an hour or more, every morning of the first week,

in explaining, fully and clearly, the principles according
to which I should manage and teach. I told them : —

" I do not believe in the necessity of corporal pun-
ishment, and I shall never strike a blow unless you
compel me. I want you to learn to govern yourselves.
I shall regard you and treat you all as young gentlemen, and expect you to consider me a gentleman, and
treat me accordingly.

" I shall always believe every word you say, until I
find you guilty of lying, and then I cannot ; nobody be-
lieves a liar, if he has any temptation to lie.

" Never tell me anything to the disadvantage of any
fellow-student. I mean to have strict rules, and to have
them strictly obeyed ; but I shall never make a rule
which I would not more willingly see broken than I
would have any one of you violate what ought to be
his feeling of honor toward a fellow-student. It is the
meanest thing that any boy can do.

" I have examined you very carefully, as you all
know, and have taken every means of finding out your
character and capacities, and your opportunities. Some
of you have enjoyed every advantage You have lived
in pleasant homes, with intelligent and well-informed
parents and friends, and you have formed habits of
reading good books, and being otherwise pleasantly
and well employed. Others of you have been blessed
with none of these privileges, and have had no opportunities of forming good habits. Now I am going to
examine you, for some weeks, carefully and severely, in
a considerable variety of studies. I shall do this that
I may arrange you according to your attainments and
capacities, so that no one may be kept back from doing

what he is capable of, and that the slow and ill-prepared may be fairly tried.

" After I shall have ascertained, in this way, of what each of you is capable, in all the studies, I shall, when I find that a dull boy has done his best, feel for him the same respect, and give him the same mark that I shall to the brightest boy in school who has only done *his* best.

" I beg of you, boys, never to try to surpass each other. Help each other in every way you can. Try to surpass yourselves. Say, ' I will do better to-day than I did yesterday, and I resolve to do better to-morrow than I can do to-day.' In this way, you who are highest and most capable will always, through life, be friends, and the best friends. But if you try to surpass each other, some of you will inevitably be enemies." *

I said this with a vivid remembrance of the bitter feelings entertained by individuals in several of the classes I had known in Cambridge, toward some of their classmates, who might have been, all their lives, their best friends, if this terribly ambitious desire of acknowledged superiority had not prevented.

These principles of action, which I have here given in a few sentences, occupied half an hour or more, every morning, for the first week. I explained and enlarged till I felt sure that I was fully understood.

When I told them I should always believe them, I could not help seeing a generous resolution fixing itself

---

* Of the correctness of this opinion, I have recently had most satisfactory evidence. Two men who had been the best scholars in school, J. J. Dixwell and J. W. Edmands, continued dear friends all their lives. •

more and more firmly in the expression of every countenance. When I enlarged upon the nobleness of refusing to betray each other, I rejoiced to see a surprised but delighted feeling of exultation on the faces of most of them, and something like inquiry on other faces. When I enlarged upon the beauty of generously helping each other, and the meanness and poor selfishness of trying to climb over others, I observed a dubious expression in some faces, as if they were trying to settle a question, and of proud satisfaction in others, as if rejoicing to see it rightly settled. When I told them that I intended to be perfectly just toward them, as soon as I knew them well enough to see what would be justice, I saw hope beaming in the eyes of some sad faces where it seemed as if it had always, till then, been a stranger.

I have always felt, as I became acquainted with my pupils, which I sought to become, as soon as I could : Here is a boy who is able to take care of himself; he only wants opportunity. But here is a poor fellow who is discouraged; he wants aid and encouragement in everything; he cannot do without me; I must win his affection; if possible, make him love me. Then he will draw near to me, and learn to rely upon me, and I shall be able to help him. I have constantly been convinced, from the time I first felt the divine character of the truths of the New Testament, that invariably the best thing to be done for every child is to educate his conscience, to make him feel the enormity and ugliness of falsehood and evil, and the preciousness and beauty of truth and good. This is the one great truth which every teacher and every parent, especially every mother, should learn, without which, indeed, no noble character can be formed. Educate the conscience.

By a careful examination of many weeks, I found what each of my pupils had done, and pretty nearly what he was capable of doing, so that I could arrange them in little classes, according to their capacity and attainments. In this way I could lead some of them to do very much more than they could have done if they had been arranged together, those who were diligent and bright and had made actual progress, with the dull boys, who were without much real attainment. This was something; I could hear lessons, but I could not, in most cases, give much instruction.

There was a single exception. I had long been acquainted with Warren Colburn, had taken many long walks with him, on which we had discussed, somewhat fully, different modes of teaching; and I had been very particularly struck by his original ideas as to the true way to teach arithmetic. He had then a private school, which occupied much of his time. I told him that if he would, beginning with the simplest numbers, write out questions in the order in which he thought they ought to be put, I would try them with my pupils, and tell him how far I agreed with him, and, if I found anything to correct or alter, I would let him know. This he was glad to do; and I gave out, according to his arrangement, all the questions in the manuscript of his first edition. I found scarcely a word to correct, and was surprised and much delighted with the successful experiment.

The effect upon my boys was most satisfactory. They soon found themselves answering instantaneously, and without difficulty, questions which, without this drill, it would have been impossible for them to answer.

This, let it be remembered, was the questions of the first edition, those given by Colburn himself. That first book was the most important step in teaching that had ever been made. The use of it, just as it was, was a blessing to every child who had to be taught. It was *mental*, acting directly upon the mind. That blessing has been forfeited in almost every subsequent edition. The book is now cruelly and stupidly put into the hands of poor children to be studied, and has altogether ceased to be *mental* arithmetic.

CHAPTER VIII.

AFTER the division of the boys, according to capacity and real attainment, was made, from careful examination, I soon found, as I have already stated, that some of them could do, satisfactorily, many times more than others, and I accordingly gave to the foremost and most capable, in addition to other studies, lessons in geometry and French, and some little of real instruction in history, illustrated by geography and chronology; and recommended, for their reading at home, the lives of some of the remarkable men of ancient and modern times. For I thought then, as I do now, that history, ancient as well as modern, is to be taught most satisfactorily and pleasantly to the young through the lives of individual men.

I required all to commit to memory, and recite every Saturday, lines from the best English poets. This, I soon found, was pleasant to nearly all of them, and improved their taste and their memory. Several of them not only became very fond of this exercise, but read with delight some of the best poetry in the language, such as that of Goldsmith, Gray, Campbell, Scott, Cowper, Byron, Bryant, and some portions of Milton.

I also gave them subjects to write upon which required observation, such as the description of a street, a single building, the harbor, a boat, a ship, the State House, the Common with its trees and cows, Charles River; and gradually, subjects that required thought, such as truthfulness, habits of industry, self-culture, procrastination, choice of friends, diligence; and I still have, carefully preserved, many creditable compositions on these subjects by members of this first class.

The faithful preparation for the performance of all my duties, in management and instruction, occupied nearly all my time, leaving me little for society. For some weeks I was well accommodated at boarding-houses, but nowhere did I find a home. The longing for one led me to apply to a very noble lady whom I had long known, and to beg her to let me become one of her family. She granted my request in the kindest manner possible. She was the widow of Rev. William Emerson, and among her sons I found William, whom I had long known and loved, the best reader, and with the sweetest voice I ever heard, and a pleasant talker: Ralph Waldo, whom I had known and admired, and whom all the world now knows almost as well as I do; Edward Bliss, the most modest and genial, the most beautiful and the most graceful speaker, a universal favorite; and Charles Chauncey, bright and ready, full of sense, ambitious of distinction, and capable of it.

There was never a more delightful family or one more sure of distinction, the intimate acquaintance with which has had a most benignant influence on my whole life; and in that family I found a home.

To enable me to vary and enlarge my instruction, the school committee obtained leave to import a few philo-

sophical instruments. Dr. Prince, of Salem, whom I
went several times to confer with, gave me aid in select-
ing and ordering them; and I soon had the pleasure of
seeing them safely arrive from London. Some of these
I used as soon as any of the boys were ready to understand and profit by them, which was very soon; so
that I was able to give some real instruction.

Most of the wooden instruments soon suffered, on
account of the dryness of our climate when compared
with that of London, and had to be repaired or somewhat changed.

I required all my boys to declaim choice selections in
prose and in poetry. This was a new thing; some of
them enjoyed it, and gradually learned to speak extremely well.

We never had any difficulty in the management of
offences. Indeed, in school, there were very few to
manage. But some difficulties arose on the playground,
in which I declined to interfere, and the settlement of
which many of the boys considered important. So I
recommended that they should form a court, before
which such cases might be tried. A judge was accordingly chosen by themselves, a jury of ten, and advocates
on each side. To qualify themselves for the performance of these duties, the boys found themselves obliged
to go into the court-rooms, and see how justice was
discovered and administered by real judges and advocates and juries. Several cases were very successfully
tried, and the decisions and awards as honestly given,
and, apparently, as justly, as they are in the courts of
the Commonwealth.

At the end of the first half-year, a public examination took place. The hall was crowded by people who wanted to see how the English Classical School was managed. I explained, in a few words, my modes of governing and of teaching, and begged them to judge for themselves. The declamation was good ; the examinations in geography, history, and French satisfactory ; the poetical recitations very gratifying. In mental arithmetic, an exhibition was made which struck everybody as wonderful. Questions were given out which few persons present would have thought it possible to answer, and which were answered fully, clearly, and instantly. The effect was such as had never been dreamed of. The applause was astounding ; and the audience separated with a conviction, in the minds of some persons, that Boston had rarely seen such a school before.

For arithmetic, my pupils were constantly drilled in Colburn's Mental, learning not much else ; and they told me that it constantly happened that, in their little dealings at the shops, they knew instantly the amount of their purchases, while the sellers had to cipher them out on their books or slates, and often made mistakes.

The most serious difficulty I had ever encountered in the management of the boys was presented by the necessity of awarding the city medals. Six medals were sent to me to be given to the six best scholars in my first class. Who were the six best? I laid the matter before the school, telling the boys that it was impossible for me to tell who best deserved the medals. To do that I ought to know who had been most faithful, who had overcome the greatest difficulties, who, struggling against nature and inadequate preparation, had made really the greatest progress. I had never had a head in any class. It would not have been difficult to guess who would have been at the head. But one who, from excellent preparation and fine natural talents, would have placed himself at the head, was really not so deserving of a medal as the boy who had overcome difficulties most successfully and improved his natural powers most faithfully.

I must assign the medals. I should do it as well as I could, but I could not be sure that I did it justly. I did, accordingly, give the medals to the six whom I considered the most deserving, and who were apparently the best scholars. This assignment gave evident satisfaction in almost every case, but there was one boy who was bitterly disappointed, and who naturally charged his disappointment to me. He never looked kindly at me from that hour ; and whenever, for years after, I met him on the street, he looked away, with a cloud on his face. If I had had one medal more, I would have given it to him. But there were only six to give. I ought to have gone to the committee and insisted upon having another to bestow ; but I did not. The poor boy, afterward a somewhat distinguished man, never forgave me, — and I never forgave myself; and I never look back upon the whole matter, I never think of him, but with pain.

My original purpose in seeking the place of principal of the English Classical School was to try the experiment of making the formation and improvement of character the leading object of the school. I taught as well as I could, but always considered this teaching of little consequence compared with that of the formation in my pupils of a single and noble character. I always began school with reading a few verses from the New Testament, pointing out the great lessons they gave and the truths they taught, and asking a blessing from the Giver of all good. To be able to speak confidently of the effect of my teaching, I must be able to look into the hearts of my pupils. Judging from appearances, the observance of order and good habits, the mutual kindness I saw, and the affectionate confidence and respect entertained toward myself, I had reason to thank God for his blessing upon my work.

CHAPTER IX.

I HAD been pleasantly and successfully employed in the English Classical School for nearly two years, when the Hon. ·William Sullivan, several of whose sons had been with me in my school in Lancaster, told me that he wanted me to teach his daughters, and that he would, if I consented, find twenty-five young ladies to be my pupils, for the instruction of whom I should be much better paid than I was then paid.

I told him I was entirely satisfied with my position, and more than satisfied with my success in an experiment in some respects new. I felt the greatest interest in my work and in the boys in the school, and should be happy to go on with them. The very reason, he said, why he wished me to take charge of his daughters was that I had been so successful in the education of boys, on· the highest and most unexceptionable principles. He considered the education of girls, on such principles, more important than that of boys, because they would have almost the entire education of their children. Most men have scarcely anything to do with the highest education of their children, even their boys. It is all left to the mothers; and if the highest education, the formation of the purest character, was desirable for all children, it must be given by the mothers. These considerations, when I came to dwell upon them, naturally produced a strong effect, and made ·me ask myself whether I should not be able to do more good as a teacher of girls than it would be possible for me to do as a teacher of boys. I consulted some of my best friends, particularly Mrs. Samuel Eliot, mother of my friend S. A. Eliot, who strongly confirmed me in an affirmative answer to the question.

Mr. Sullivan soon saw, for we discussed the matter many times, that an impression had been made on me, and sought to make his argument irresistible by telling me that he knew I wanted to marry, and I might easily· see that I could not live, as I should desire to live, on the $1,500 a year I received from the city of Boston. Twenty-five girls would secure a thousand more, with which addition I might live very pleasantly. This argument convinced me, and I told him that if I could persuade Solomon P. Miles, who had succeeded me in Lancaster and in Harvard College, and had given complete satisfaction, to be a candidate for the place of master in the English Classical School, I would accept his offer. So I went out to Cambridge to see my old friend, and easily persuaded him to offer himself as the candidate.

At the same time that Mr. Sullivan was urging me, his friend, Josiah Quincy, then mayor of the city, said he would venture to promise me, if I would remain, an addition of $500 to my salary, which would make it equal to the highest salary then given to any teacher in New England. The final arrangement was concluded in April, 1823.

5

When it was known that twenty-five young ladies, from some of the best families in Boston, were to form a new school, several others were desirous of joining them, so that, on the 9th of June, 1823, thirty-two young ladies met me as pupils in a very large room in what was then a boarding-house on Beacon Street. I limited my number to thirty-two, because I thought that number as large as I could properly teach. I opened a book for applicants and entered several names, in the order of application, to be admitted in that order, as vacancies should occur in my school. This book was never without names but once as long as I kept my school. I was sitting, one Saturday evening, thinking that I should have to begin, on Monday morning, with thirty-one. This, I thought, was probably the beginning of the end; but I tried to comfort myself by thinking that, if this school failed, I could go into the country and teach boys, in a public or private school or academy. I had just come to this conclusion when a very respectable gentleman came in, full, he said, of anxiety lest he had come too late to get his daughter admitted. From that day I was never without more applicants than I could admit.

My object was, naturally, to give my pupils the best education possible, to teach them what it was most important for every one to know, and to form right habits of thought, and give such instruction as would lead to the formation of the highest character, to fit them to be good daughters and sisters, good neighbors, good wives, and good mothers. I wished to give them, as far as possible, a complete knowledge of our rich and beautiful English language. With this in view I set them all to study Latin, since all the hardest words in our language, as in French and Italian, are thence derived. Some fathers begged me not to let their daughters waste their time upon Latin, but rather devote it to French and Italian. All such girls I set immediately to study French. But to the rest I gave four or five lessons every week in the Latin language, with as little as possible of the grammar. I kept up this for two years always, and in some cases for three. At the end of the two or three Latin years, I set them to study French and then Italian. These studies were very easy, as they found that they knew already the roots of nearly all the hard words, and so could give much of their time to writing the languages.

At the end of three or four years, those who had studied Latin knew more of French and Italian than those who had given all their time to them. In Italian, those who had studied Virgil faithfully, found little difficulty with Dante, who had followed Virgil so far as language alone was in question, and whose language is more like Virgil's Latin than it is like modern Italian. Those who had studied only French and Italian, found Dante almost unintelligible, and were, nearly all of them, obliged to give him up. Many years afterwards, I spent half a year in Rome, and became acquainted with some of the teachers. They told me they never thought of setting their pupils to read Dante. It was almost unintelligible to them.

For arithmetic, my pupils were constantly drilled in Colburn's Mental, learning not much else; and they told me that it constantly happened that, in their little dealings at the shops, they knew instantly the amount of their purchases, while the sellers had to cipher them out on their books or slates, and often made mistakes.

In history, I began and long continued in the old way, giving out six or eight pages in some excellent writer, such as Robertson, and requiring my pupils to answer the questions I put to them at the next morning's recitation. This was more satisfactory to some of them than to me, so that, after some years, I undertook to teach them history in another way. On warm days in summer, for the school then stretched into summer, I set them all down with their maps before them, and for one or two hours, gave them, in my own words, what I considered the most interesting and important facts and thoughts in a portion of history, sometimes, however, reading long passages when they were clear and well written.

This made them familiar with the authors I quoted, and often led to a more intimate acquaintance. In the two months during which this reading was continued, not much history could be given, but a love for it was formed which led to pleasant reading, by themselves, of many favorite volumes, and to the habit of reading good books, which has, in many instances, lasted always.

In natural philosophy, I began with the easiest text-books I could find, and with a few experiments making things clear and creating an interest. These early books were English, and very excellent. When I had to use American, I soon found that they were usually the poor abridgments of larger treatises, made by ignorant persons, for the printer. The apparent originals I found little better, made by illiterate people, for sale in the schools and academies. This drove me to the real originals, so that I was led to read Newton's *Principia*, La Place, Galileo, Lavoisier, and other books, the works of the original thinkers. To do this required an immense deal of time, so that I was actually driven into the habit of never going abroad to spend my evenings, with the single exception of one evening in a week, to meet at a club a small number of very old friends.

CHAPTER X.

GRADUALLY other things, of a more public nature, came in to occupy and diversify my thoughts. I had become acquainted with some of the common schools in the State, and met with individuals, teachers and others, who were acquainted with them, and sympathized with me in regard to their wretched condition. For several years we met, in Boston, every summer, to talk about them, and to consider whether something could not be done for their improvement, and at last concluded that a society of teachers should be formed, the one object of which should be the improvement of the common schools.

BOSTON SOCIETY OF NATURAL HISTORY.

In the winter of 1830 a few gentlemen of scientific attainments conceived the design of forming a society in Boston for the promotion of natural history. After several meetings, usually held in the office of Dr. Walter Channing, and communicating their design to others supposed or known to be favorably disposed toward it. a meeting in the same place was called, on the 28th of April, 1830. It was organized by the choice of Dr. Channing as moderator, and Theophilus Parsons, Esq., as secretary. The gentlemen present then resolved to form themselves into a society, under the name of the Boston Society of Natural History. A constitution and by-laws were adopted, officers were chosen, an act of incorporation was obtained, at the next session of the Legislature, bearing date February 24, 1831.

The great object had in view in the formation of the society was to promote a taste, and afford facilities, for the pursuit of natural history, by mutual co-operation, and the formation of a cabinet and a library. But it was always understood that especial attention should be given to the investigation of the objects in our own immediate vicinity.

Thomas Nuttall, Esq., the well-known botanist and ornithologist, was chosen the first president; but, regarding himself as only a transient resident, he declined the office, to which Benj. D. Greene, a distinguished botanist, was chosen. Among those most early interested were Drs. Geo. Hayward and John Ware, Hon. F. C. Gray, Rev. F. W. P. Greenwood, Charles T. Jackson, M. D., Dr. D. Humphreys Storer, Dr. Augustus A. Gould. To Dr. Gould's notice of these events I am indebted for almost all that I have here recorded.

A few of us, from the beginning, often met and discussed the character of the natural objects that presented themselves. We continued, for some years, to meet, often, in the evening, at each other's houses. In 1837 I was chosen president. We had then made valuable collections, by gifts and our own researches. These collections of our own we found seldom anywhere described, and, talking these things over, many times, we at last concluded that a survey of the whole State ought to be made, by competent persons, to complete the excellent

Report made by Dr. Hitchcock upon the mineralogy and geology of the State, and that it was our duty to lay this want before the government of the State, and to endeavor to have a survey organized.

As I was president, it was agreed that I ought to write a memorial and lay it before Gov. Everett. This I accordingly did, as well as I could

Gov. Everett, who was an old friend of mine, received my memorial very graciously, and read it. He said that he was very glad that I had written the memorial, that he coincided in the statements therein made, and that he would immediately lay it before the Senate and the House of Representatives.

In a few days he sent for me, and told me that my memorial had been very justly appreciated by both houses, who had given him authority to appoint six persons to make a survey of the State, and had voted an appropriation for the expenses of the survey. "Now," he said, "you are better acquainted with the naturalists in the State than I am, and will do me a favor by suggesting the names of persons whom you consider competent to do this work satisfactorily." I told him I knew some such persons; that Dr. Harris, of Cambridge, was a very learned entomologist, and knew the nature and the habits of more insects than any other person in the country. Dr. Harris was agreed upon as the most suitable person to report upon the insects. I told him Dr. Gould was a very nice observer, an excellent draughtsman and dissector, and well acquainted with many of the lower animals. He was accordingly appointed to report on invertebrates. Dr. Storer was a careful observer, and had already become acquainted with many of the fishes of the sea and rivers. Dr. Storer was appointed to make a report upon the fishes. There was another person, I told him, who knew more about the birds than any other person in the country. " Stop there!" said Gov. Everett. "Will it do, in providing for a survey of the State of Massachusetts, to appoint men from Boston and Cambridge only?" I told him I was not intimately acquainted with the naturalists in other parts of the State ; I only knew them by report. "How would Mr. Peabody, of Springfield, do for the birds?" asked he. I answered that I knew Mr. Peabody, as he knew him, as a person of very great talent, and an admirable writer. If he knew nothing especially about the birds, he could soon find out, and then he would write a report so well that everybody would be charmed with it. Mr. Peabody was accordingly appointed to write a report upon the birds. Then Gov. Everett asked, "Do you not know men, in the extreme west, in Berkshire, at Stockbridge, or Williamstown?" "There is," I said, "a man at Stockbridge who must be a good botanist ; he has just given, in Silliman's *Journal*, one or two excellent papers upon the sedges, one of the most difficult genera in botany." "Well, let Dr. Dewey report upon botany." Then I said, "I do not know who is the Professor of Natural History in Williams College, but I do know President Hopkins, and am pretty sure that he would not appoint a very ordinary man." Prof. Emmons was accordingly appointed to report upon the quadrupeds.

When I met my friends in the society, and told them what names I had suggested, they immediately asked to what I was myself to be appointed. I answered, "To none ; Gov. Everett has made me responsible for all the reports; I must read them, and see them through the press. Besides, I have not the time, for you all know that, for nine months in the year, I am as busy as possible with my school." "That will not do," they responded; "we have all been accustomed to work with you, and who else would be so pleasant to work with?" So they continued to urge. I told them all the places were filled, just the six we had agreed upon. "Why cannot you," one of them insisted, "agree with Dr. Dewey to divide the botany, he taking all the other plants, and giving you the trees and shrubs, of which you know more than any of us? *They* will be enough for one person." So they compelled me to yield. I wrote to Prof. Dewey, who answered me immediately that he should rejoice to give the trees to some one else, as he did not know them very well, and could hardly find time to study them.

I was thus pressed into the work, which, however, I resolved to do as well as I could make myself able to do. For ten or twelve weeks of nine successive summers, I devoted myself to the exploration. I visited and explored every considerable forest in the State. I wrote to several hundreds of those known or supposed to be acquainted with the woods, and received very many valuable letters. I thus became acquainted with nearly every variety of tree, and studied it attentively. I was in the habit of sitting down under a tree, to examine it, root, stem, bark, branches, leaves, and fruits, as thoroughly as I could, recording all that I saw. In many instances I compared my notes, made in one part of the State, with what I had observed in another, a hundred miles off.

I thus became acquainted, as thoroughly as I was able,

with all the trees and shrubs in the State. This was very pleasant work, and I made acquaintance, far more pleasant, with the farmers in every part of the State. They were always willing and glad to leave their own work and walk with me, often all day long, through the woods, showing me the remarkable trees, and hearing from me their names. I never received an unkind or discourteous answer from a farmer in any part of the State, except once, within three miles of Boston, and that was from an Englishman.

Most of the reports were sent in within a year. That by Mr. Peabody, upon the birds, was charmingly written, and was read with gratification by all lovers of birds. It undoubtedly saved the lives of thousands, and turned the attention of the agricultural population to the valuable services they perform.

Dr. Harris's report, upon insects injurious to vegetation, was admitted at once, by those acquainted with the subject, to be the most valuable report ever made. It has been again and again republished by the Legislature. In the last edition, illustrated with figures, it takes its place among the very best reports ever made upon the subject.

Dr. Gould's report was confined to the shells, and was the first report upon that subject ever made in this country. He gives a very accurate, often extremely beautiful figure of every object described, and an equally excellent description. With the aid of his book, any careful observer may find out the nature and character of every shell. This report was published in 1841.

Dr. Gould was engaged in preparing a fuller and more complete report, which was interrupted by death in

1866, and his work was satisfactorily completed by his friend, W. G. Binney.

Dr. Storer's report upon the fishes and reptiles of Massachusetts was given to me, with that upon the birds, and by me laid before Gov. Everett in 1839, and immediately printed for the benefit of the inhabitants.

CHAPTER XI.

FOR several years the condition of the common schools in New England was very often a subject of conversation at the annual meetings of the American Institute of Instruction. It was unanimously agreed that these schools were in a desperately low condition, and yet growing worse from year to year. At last it was determined that something ought to be done for their improvement, and that the directors of the Institute ought to do it; and it was resolved that a memorial upon the subject should be made to the Legislature, and that I, being president, ought to prepare and to offer it. This was done, and the following memorial was placed in the hands of the governor, with a request that he would lay it before the Senate and House of Representatives: —

MEMORIAL OF THE AMERICAN INSTITUTE OF INSTRUC-
TION TO THE MASSACHUSETTS LEGISLATURE.

To the Honorable the Legislature of the Commonwealth of Mass. :

The memorial of the Directors of the American Institute of Instruction, praying that provision may be made for the better preparation of the teachers of the schools of the Commonwealth, respectfully showeth :

That there is, throughout the Commonwealth, a great want of well-qualified teachers ;

That this is felt in all the schools, of all classes, but especially in the most important and numerous class, the District Schools ;

That wherever, in any town, exertion has been made to improve these schools, it has been met and baffled by the want of good teachers ; that they have been sought for in vain ; the highest salaries have been offered to no purpose ; that they are *not to be found* in sufficient numbers to supply the demand ;

That their place is supplied by persons exceedingly incompetent, in *many* respects ; by young men, in the course of their studies, teaching from necessity, and often with a strong dislike for the pursuit ; by mechanics and others wanting present employment ; and by persons who have failed in other callings and take to teaching as a last resort, with no qualification for it, and no desire of continuing in it longer than they are obliged by an absolute necessity ;

That those among this number who have a natural fitness for the work, now gain the experience — without which no one, whatever his gifts, can become a good teacher — by the sacrifice, winter after winter, of the time and advancement of the children of the schools of the Commonwealth ;

That every school is now liable to have a winter's session wasted by the unskilful attempts of an instructor making his first experiments in teaching. By the close of the season, he may have gained some insight into the mystery, may have hit upon some tolerable method of discipline, may have grown somewhat familiar with the books used and with the character of the children ; and, if he could go on in the same school for successive years, might become a profitable teacher. But whatever he may have gained *himself* from his experiments, he will have failed too entirely of meeting the just expectations of the district to leave him any hope of being engaged for a second term. He accordingly looks elsewhere for the next season, and the district receives another master, to have the existing regulations set aside, and to undergo another series of experiments. We do not state the fact too strongly, when we say that *the time, capacities, and opportunities of thousands of the children are sacrificed, winter after winter*, to the preparation of teachers who, after this enormous sacrifice, are, notwithstanding, often very wretchedly prepared ;

That many times no preparation is even aimed at ; that such is the known demand for teachers of every kind, with or without qualifications, that candidates present themselves for the employment, and committees, in despair of finding better, employ those who have no degree of fitness for the work ; that committees are obliged to employ, to take charge of their children, men to whose incompetency they would reluctantly commit their farms or their workshops ;

That the reaction of this deplorable incompetency of the teachers upon the minds of the committees is hardly less to be deplored, hardly less alarming, as it threatens to continue the evil and render it perpetual. Finding they cannot get suitable teachers at any price, they naturally apportion the salary to the value of the service rendered, and the consequence is that, in many places, the wages of a teacher are below those given in the humblest of the mechanic arts ; and instances are known of persons of tolerable qualifications as teachers declining to quit, for a season, some of the least gainful of the trades, on the ground of the lowness of the teacher's pay.

We merely state these facts, without enlarging upon them, as they have too great and melancholy a notoriety. We but add our voice to the deep tone of grief and complaint which sounds from every part of the Commonwealth. We are not surprised at this condition of the teachers ; we should be surprised if it were much otherwise.

Most of the winter schools are taught for about three months of the year, the summer not far beyond four. They are therefore of necessity taught, and must continue to be taught, by persons who, for two thirds or three fourths of the year, have other pursuits, in qualifying themselves for which they have spent the usual period, and which, of course, they look upon as the main business of their lives. They cannot be expected to make great exertions and expensive preparation for the work of teaching, in which the standard is so low, and for which they are so poorly paid.

Whatever desire they might have, it would be almost in vain. There are now no places suited to give them the instruction they need. For every other profession, requiring a knowledge of the principles of science and the conclusions of experience, there are special schools and colleges, with learned and able professors and ample apparatus. For the preparation of the teacher, there is almost none. In every other art ministering to the wants and convenience of men, masters may be found ready to impart whatsoever of skill they have to the willing apprentice; and the usage of society justly requires that years should be spent, under the eye of an adept, to gain the requisite ability. An apprenticeship to a schoolmaster is known only in tradition. We respectfully maintain that it ought not so to be. So much of the intelligence and character, the welfare and immediate and future happiness of all the citizens, now and hereafter, depends on the condition of the common schools, that it is of necessity a matter of the dearest interest to all the present generation; that the common education is to such a degree the palladium of our liberties, and the good condition of the common schools, in which that education is chiefly obtained, so vitally important to the *stability* of our State, to our very *existence* as a *free* State, that it is the most proper subject for legislation, and calls loudly for legislative provision and protection. The commons schools ought to be raised to their proper place, and this can only be done by the better education of the teachers.

We maintain that provision ought to be made, by the *Stat*, for the education of teachers; *because*, while their education is so important to the State, their condition generally is such as to put a suitable education entirely beyond their reach; *because*, by no other means is it likely that a system shall be introduced which shall prevent the immense annual loss of time to the schools from a change of teachers; and *because* the qualifications of a first-rate teacher are such as cannot be gained but by giving a considerable time wholly to the work of preparation.

In his calling there is a peculiar difficulty in the fact that, whereas, in other callings and professions, duties

6

and difficulties come on gradually, and one by one, giving ample time in the intervals for special preparation, in *his* they all come at once. On the first day on which he enters the school, his difficulties meet him with a single, unbroken, serried front, as numerously as they ever will; and they refuse to be separated. He cannot divide and overcome them singly, putting off the more formidable to wrestle with at a future time. He could only have met them with complete success by long forecast, by months and years of preparation.

The qualifications requisite in a good teacher, of which many have so low and inadequate an idea as to think them almost the instinctive attributes of every man and every woman, we maintain to be noble and excellent qualities, rarely united in a high degree in the same individual, and to obtain which one *must* give, and may *well* give, much time and study.

We begin with the *lowest.* He must have a *thorough knowledge* of whatever he undertakes to teach. If it were not so common, how absurd would it seem that one should undertake to communicate to another fluency and grace in the beautiful accomplishment of reading, without having them himself; or to give skill in the processes of arithmetic, while he understands them so dimly himself as to be obliged to follow the rules as blindly as the child he is teaching. And yet are there not many teachers yearly employed by committees, from the impossibility of finding better, who, in reading and arithmetic, as in everything else, are but one step before, if they do not fall behind, the foremost of their own pupils? Is it not so in geography, in English grammar, in everything, in short, which is now required to be taught? If the teacher understood thoroughly what is required in the usual prescribed course, it would be *something.* But we maintain that the teachers of the public schools ought to be able to t_o do *much more.* In every school occasions are daily occurring, on which, from a well-stored mind, could be imparted, upon the most interesting and important subjects, much that, at the impressible period of his pupilage, would be of the greatest value to the learner. Besides, there are always at least a few forward pupils, full of talent, ready to make advances far beyond the common course. Such, if their teacher could conduct them, would rejoice, instead of circling again and again in the same dull round, to go *onward,* in other and higher studies, so manifestly valuable that the usual studies of a school seem but as steps intended to lead up to them.

In the second place, a teacher should so understand the *ordering* and *discipline* of a school as to be able at once to introduce system, and keep it constantly in force. Much precious time, as already stated, is lost in making, changing, abrogating, modelling, and re-modelling rules and regulations. And not only is the time *utterly lost*, but the changes are a source of *perplexity* and *vexation* to master and pupil. A judicious system of regulations not only takes up no time, but *saves* time for everything else. We believe there are few persons to whom this knowledge of system comes without an effort, who are *born* with such an aptitude to order that they fall into it naturally and of course.

In the third place, a teacher should know *how* to teach. This, we believe, is the rarest and most important of his qualifications. Without it, great knowledge, however pleasant to the possessor, will be of little use to his pupils ; and with it, a small fund will be made to produce great effects. It cannot with propriety be considered a single faculty. It is rather a practical knowledge of the best methods of bringing the truths of the several subjects that are to be taught to the comprehension of the learner. Not often does the same method apply to several studies. It must vary with the nature of the truths to be communicated, and with the age, capacity, and advancement of the pupil. To possess it fully, one must have ready command of elementary principles, a habit of seeing them in various points of view, and promptly seizing the one best suited to the learner ; a power of awakening his curiosity, and of adapting the lessons to the mind, so as to bring out its faculties naturally and without violence. It therefore supposes an acquaintance with the *minds* of children, the order in which their faculties expand, and by what discipline they may be nurtured, and their inequalities repaired.

This knowledge of the human mind and character may be stated as a fourth qualification of a teacher. Without it he will be always groping his way darkly. He will disgust the forward and quick-witted by making them linger along with the slow, and dishearten the slow by expecting them to keep pace with the swift. Whoever considers to how great a degree the successful action of the mind depends on the state of the feelings and affections, will be ready to admit that an instructor should know so much of the connection and subordination of the parts of the human character as to be able to enlist them all in the same cause, to gain the *heart* to the side of advancement, and to make the *affections* the ministers of truth and wisdom.

CHAPTER XII.

MEMORIAL OF THE AMERICAN INSTITUTE OF INSTRUC-
TION TO THE MASSACHUSETTS LEGISLATURE. (CON-
CLUDED.)

W E have spoken very briefly of some of the qualifications essential to a good teacher. It is
hardly necessary to say that there are still higher qualifications which ought to belong to the persons who are
to have such an influence upon the character and well-
being of the future citizens of the Commonwealth, who,
besides parents, can do more than all others toward
training the young to a clear perception of right and
wrong, to the love of truth, to reverence for the laws
of man and of God, to the performance of all the
duties of good citizens and good men. The teacher
ought to be a person of elevated character, able to win
by his manners and instruct by his example, *without* as
well as *within* the school.

Now, it is known to your memorialists that a very
large number of those, of both sexes, who now teach
the summer and the winter schools, are, *to a mournful
degree*, wanting in all these qualifications. Far from
being able to avail themselves of opportunities of communicating knowledge on various subjects, they are
grossly ignorant of what they are called on to teach.

They are often without experience in managing a
school ; they have no skill in communicating. Instead
of being able to stimulate and guide to all that is noble
and excellent, they are, not seldom, persons of such
doubtful respectability and refinement of character that
no one would think for a moment of holding them up
as models to their pupils. In short, they know not
what to teach, nor *how* to teach, nor in *what spirit* to
teach, nor what is the nature of *those* they undertake to
lead, nor what they are *themselves* who stand forward to
lead them.

Your memorialists believe that these are evils *of por-
tentous moment* to the future welfare of the people of
this Commonwealth, and that, while they bear heavily
on all, they bear especially and with disproportioned
weight upon the poorer districts in the scattered population of the country towns. The wealthy are less
directly affected by them, as they can send their children from home to the better schools in other places.
The large towns are not affected in the same degree, as
their density of population enables them to employ
teachers through the year, at salaries which command
somewhat high qualifications.

We believe that you have it in your power to adopt
such measures as shall forthwith diminish these evils,
and at last remove them ; and that this can only be
done by providing for the better preparation of teachers. We therefore pray you to consider the expediency
of instituting, for the special instruction of teachers,
one or more seminaries, — either standing independ-
ently, or in connection with institutions already existing, — as you shall, in your wisdom, think best. We

also beg leave to state what we conceive to be essential to such a seminary.

1. There should be a professor or professors, of piety, of irreproachable character and good education, and of tried ability and skill in teaching ;

2. A library, not necessarily large, but well chosen, of books on the subjects to be taught and on the art of teaching ;

3. School-rooms well situated and arranged, heated, ventilated, and furnished in the manner best approved by experienced teachers ;

4. A select apparatus of globes, maps, and other instruments most useful for illustration ;

5. A situation such that a school may be connected with the seminary, accessible by a sufficient number of children to give the variety of an ordinary district school.

We beg leave, also, further, to state the manner in which we conceive that such a seminary would be immediately useful to the schools within the sphere of its influence. We do not believe that the majority of the district schools in the Commonwealth will soon, if ever, be taught by permanent teachers ; we believe that they will continue to be taught, as they are now, by persons who, for the greater part of the year, will be engaged in some other pursuit ; that as, in the early history of Rome, the generous husbandman left his plough to fight the battles of the state, so in Massachusetts, the free and intelligent citizen will, for a time, quit his business, his workshop, or his farm, to fight, for the sake of his children and the State, a more vital battle against immorality and ignorance. And we rejoice to believe that it will be so. So shall the hearts of the fathers be in the schools of their children ; so shall the teachers have that knowledge of the world, that acquaintance with men and things, so often wanting in the mere school-master, and yet not among the least essential of his qualifications. But we wish to see these citizens enjoy the means of obtaining the knowledge and practical skill in the art of teaching which shall enable them to perform the duties of this additional office worthily.

Establish a seminary wherever you please, and it will be immediately resorted to. We trust too confidently in that desire of excellence which seems to be an element in our New England character, to doubt that any young man, who, looking forward, sees that he shall have occasion to teach a school every winter for ten years, will avail himself of any means within his reach of preparation for the work. Give him the opportunity, and he cannot fail to be essentially benefited by his attendance at the seminary, if it be but for a *single month.*

In the first place, he will see there an example of right ordering and management of a school, the spirit of which he may immediately imbibe, and can never after be at a loss as to a *model* of management, or in doubt as to its *importance.*

In the second place, by listening to the teaching of another, he will be convinced of the necessities of preparation, as he will see that success depends on thorough knowledge and a direct action of the teacher's own mind. This alone would be a great point, as many a school-master hears reading and spelling, and

looks over writing and arithmetic, without ever attempt-
ing to give any instruction or explanation, or even
thinking them necessary.

In the third place, he will see put in practice methods
of teaching ; and though he may, on reflection, conclude
that none of them are exactly suited to his own mind,
he will see the value of method, and will never after
proceed as he would have done if he had never seen
methodical teaching at all.

In the next place, he will have new light thrown
upon the whole work of education, by being made to
perceive that its great end is not mechanically to communicate ability in certain operations, but to draw forth
and exercise the whole powers of the physical, intel-
lectual, and moral being.

He will, moreover, hardly fail to observe the importance of the *manners* of an instructor, and how far it
depends on himself to give a tone of cheerfulness and
alacrity to his school.

In the last place, if the right spirit prevails at the
seminary, he will be prepared to enter upon his office
with an exalted sense of its importance and responsi-
bility, not as a poor drudge performing a loathsome
office for a miserable stipend, but as a delegate of the
authority of parents and the state, to form men to the
high duties of citizens and the infinite destinies of
immortality, answerable to them, their country, and
their God for the righteous discharge of his duties.

Now, we believe that this single month's preparation
would be of immense advantage to a young instructor.
Let him now enter the district school. He has a definite idea what arrangements he is to make, what course

he is to pursue, what he is to take hold of first. He knows that he is himself to teach ; he knows what to teach, and, in some measure, how he is to set about it. He feels how much he has to do to prepare himself, and how much depends on his self-preparation. He has some conception of the duties and requirements of his office. At the end of a single season he will, we venture to say, be a better teacher than he could have been after half a dozen, had he not availed himself of the experience of others. He will hardly fail to seek future occasions to draw more largely at the same fountain.

Let us not be understood as offering this statement of probable results as mere conjecture. They have been confirmed by all the experience, to the point, of a single institution in this State, and of many in a foreign country. What is thus, from experience and the reason of things, shown to be true in regard to a short preparation, will be still more strikingly so of a longer one. To him who shall make teaching the occupation of his life, the advantages of a teacher's seminary cannot easily be estimated. They can be faintly imagined by him only, who, lawyer, mechanic, or physician, can figure to himself what would have been his feelings, had he, on the first day of his apprenticeship, been called to perform at once all the difficult duties of his future profession, and after being left to suffer for a time the agony of despair at the impossibility, had been told that two, three, seven years should be allowed him to prepare himself, with all the helps and appliances which are now so bountifully *furnished* to him, which are furnished to *every one* except the teacher.

We have no doubt that teachers prepared at such a seminary would be in such request as to command at once higher pay than is now given, since it would unquestionably be found good economy to employ them.

It raises no objection in the minds of your memorialists, to the plan of a seminary at the State's expense, that many of the instructors there prepared would teach for only a portion of the year. It is *on that very ground* that they ought to be aided. For their daily callings they will take care to qualify themselves; they cannot, unaided, be expected to do the same in regard to the office of teacher, because it is a casual and temporary one. It is one which they will exercise, in the intervals of their stated business, for the good of their fellow-citizens. They ought, for that especial reason, to be assisted in preparing for it. The gain will be theirs, it is true, but it will be still more the gain of the community. It will be theirs, inasmuch as they will be able to command better salaries; but it will be only in consideration of the more valuable service they will render.

The gain will be shared by other schools than those they teach. Seeing what can be done by *good* teachers, districts and committees will no longer rest satisfied with poor, and the standard will everywhere rise.

If it were only as enabling teachers throughout the State to teach, as they should, the branches now required to be taught, the seminaries would be worth more than their establishment can cost. But they would do much more. They would render the instruction given more worthy, in kind and degree, the enlightened citizens of a free State.

Without going too minutely into this part of the subject, we cannot fully show how the course of instruction might, in our judgment, be enlarged. We may be
allowed to indicate a few particulars.

The study of geometry, that benignant nurse of
inventive genius, is at present pursued partially in a
few of the town schools. We may safely assert that,
under efficient teachers, the time now given to arithmetic would be amply sufficient, not only for that, but
for geometry and its most important applications in
surveying and other useful arts. To a population so
full of mechanical talent as ours, this would be a precious gain.

We may also point to the case of drawing in right
lines. It might, with a saving of time, be ingrafted on
writing, if the instructors were qualified to teach it.
This beautiful art, so valuable as a guide to the hand
and eye of every one, especially of every handicrafts-
man, and deemed almost an essential in every school
of France and other countries of Europe, is, so far as
we can learn from the secretary's excellent Report,
entirely neglected in every public school in Massachusetts.

We might make similar observations in regard to
book-keeping, now beginning to be introduced; to natural philosophy, physiology, natural history, and other
studies which might come in, not to the exclusion, but
to the manifest improvement of the studies already
pursued.

When we consider the many weeks in our long Northern winters, during which, all through our borders, the
arts of the husbandman and builder seem, like the pro-

cesses of the vegetable world, to hold holiday, and the
sound of many a trowel and many an axe and hammer
ceases to be heard, and that the hours, without any
interruption of the busy labors of the year, might be
given to learning by the youth of both sexes, almost up
to the age of maturity, these *omissions*, the *unemployed
intellect*, the golden days of early manhood *lost*, the
acquisitions that *might* be made and *are not*, assume a
vastness of importance which may well alarm us.

It may possibly be apprehended that should superior
teachers be prepared in the seminaries of Massachusetts, they would be invited to other States by higher
salaries, and the advantage of their education be thus
lost to the State.

We know not that it ought to be considered an unde-
sirable thing that natives of Massachusetts, who will
certainly go from time to time to regions more favored
by nature, should go with such characters and endowments as to render their chosen homes more worthy to
be the residence of intelligent men. But we apprehend
it to be an event much more likely to happen that the
successful example of Massachusetts should be imitated
by her sister republics, emulous, as New York has
already shown herself, to surpass us in what has hither-
to been the chief glory of New England, — a jealous
care of the public schools.

For the elevation of the public schools to the high
rank which they ought to hold in a community whose
most precious patrimony is their liberty, and the intelligence, knowledge, and virtue on which alone it can
rest, we urge our prayer. We speak boldly, for we
seek no private end. We speak in the name and

behalf of those who cannot appear before you to urge their own suit, — the sons and daughters of the present race, and of all, of every race and class, of coming generations in all future times.

For the Directors of the American Institute of Instruction.

$$\left.\begin{array}{l} \text{GEO. B. EMERSON,} \\ \text{S. R. HALE.} \\ \text{W. J. ADAMS,} \\ \text{D. KIMBALL,} \\ \text{E. A. ANDREWS,} \\ \text{B. GREENLEAF,} \\ \text{N. CLEAVELAND,} \end{array}\right\} \textit{Committee.}$$

CHAPTER XIII.

THE effect of this communication was immediate and very decided. All other business, in both Houses, was given up, and the attention of all was given to the question, How shall the schools of the Commonwealth be improved ? A Board of Education was formed, and Horace Mann, president of the Senate and the ablest man in both Houses, was unanimously chosen secretary, on a salary of $1,500. This appointment he accepted, with the understanding that he should give his whole time and attention to the duties of the office. He thus relinquished at once his business as a lawyer, which, in Boston alone, would have been at least $15,000 for the next year.

The Board of Education speedily resolved that there should be a Normal School for the preparation of teachers, and Mr. Mann looked everywhere for a capable person to be the head of this school. He found that the boys who filled the office of apprentice in the places of business in Nantucket, understood and performed their duty better and more intelligently than those in any other place, and that all these boys were or had been taught by one individual, the faithful, well-educated, and intelligent Cyrus Pierce, who was accordingly made head of the first Normal School   This was opened in Lexington, the generous inhabitants of which town had offered to the State a building for the purpose, which was amply sufficient for the beginning. The Hon. Edmund Dwight, who had generously added $1,000 to the salary of Horace Mann, and who had, in various ways, shown the deep interest he felt in the education of the State, accompanied me to Lexington, to make the first visit to Mr. Pierce. We found him in a comfortable little room, with two pupils, a third being necessarily absent. He received us very cordially, and assured us that he was pleasantly situated and full of hope.

I continued to feel a strong interest in the schools of the Commonwealth, and visited the Normal Schools, for many years, more frequently than any other individual. I found, in West Newton, a suitable building, into which the school was transferred when that at Lexington had ceased to be large enough, and some years after, selected, in the very centre of the State at Lexington, a site for a Normal School, and drew the plan of the building erected there. I continued to visit the schools, especially those at Bridgewater, Salem, and West Newton, and did everything I could for them, sometimes aiding in the examination for admission of pupils.

I had been, for more than forty years, most pleasantly engaged in teaching, always successful, and always giving satisfaction to my pupils and engaging their affections, when my best friends came to the conclusion that I was wearing out, and that it was not safe for me to continue longer in the uninterrupted work, however pleasant it might be.

I therefore yielded to their importunities, and con-

7

sented to give up my school, and to go abroad for two
years. There were a thousand things in Europe that
it would be delightful to see and to know, which I was
well prepared to enjoy, especially as I had made myself thoroughly acquainted with the French and Italian
languages, and had made some progress in the German.

After careful preparation we, that is, my wife and
myself, embarked on board an excellent steamer, and
had a very pleasant voyage to Liverpool. I was fond
of the sea, and perfectly prepared to enjoy it, but my
wife suffered very much, so that she could not, after the
first two days, be upon deck, but remained always in
her berth. She was, however, entirely relieved in two
days after landing at Liverpool, and we began with the
pleasant old town of Chester, which we found full of
interest. We walked round it on the walls, and saw
everything in its neighborhood, especially the exquisite
old cemetery, which was charmingly situated in a vast,
irregular cavity which had been made in the sandstone
from which the walls and the buildings of the old town
had been taken. We thought it the most beautiful
cemetery we had ever seen, and we think so still, after
having seen very many others in every part of Europe.

Chester is entirely unlike every other town we visited.
On each side of most of the streets, the passage for
ladies is raised eight or nine feet above the ground, and
all the pleasant shops open along it, leaving the en-
trances below for fuel and all other heavy or disagreeable
supplies.

The views from the walls are extremely rich and
varied, and interesting for the very important events

that have occurred in this neighborhood for many years, an account of which would fill many a volume.

We examined with interest the old cathedral, as we did afterwards nearly all the best, old, as well as the comparatively new cathedrals, in every part of the island.

We carefully examined every part of old Haddon Hall, which gave a very satisfactory idea of the buildings of former times ; and then drove to Chatsworth, by way of the park, in which there were said to be sixteen hundred deer, besides many other animals. The oaks, beeches, ashes, limes, thorns, and chestnuts are magnificent. The house itself is a stately palace, to describe the entrance hall, the staircases, passages, galleries, and state-rooms of which would require a volume. So the gardens and grounds. Here were all the pines then known. The glass house, seventy feet high, was full of exotics, the largest and rarest that have been collected, a cocoa-palm seventy feet high, sago-trees, dracænas, cactuses, black and yellow cane-poles, all as luxuriant as if growing in their natural *habitat.* The collection of ferns was vast and wonderful.

The rock-work, all artificial and all seeming natural ; the cascades and *jets d'eau*, the French gardens so exact, the Italian so stately and magnificent, the English, so surpassing everything else ! Among the many gardens we saw afterward, we saw nothing superior to this, and we saw all that were most famous, and everything most interesting in the island.

In Cambridge I saw the room in which Milton is said to have dwelt when an undergraduate, " Lycidas " and other things in his own handwriting, and the ruinous old mulberry-tree which he is said to have planted.

At London we saw the Crystal Palace and its wonders; in Paris, a great show that they called the Exposition, containing everything most beautiful and most characteristic of the fine arts, especially those that are interesting to ladies of the most delicate tastes.

In Paris I heard many admirable lectures by distinguished men, on a great variety of subjects. We saw a large part of France. Nothing was more interesting than the forest, extending more than a hundred miles along the southwest coast and from six to eighteen into the interior, formed by the skill and sagacity of an individual influencing the action of the French government; and nothing more delightful than the journey by land, along the coast of the Gulf of Genoa. We spent four months in Rome, long enough to see everything most interesting in the city and its neighborhood, and to become acquainted with all the plants. Not less pleasant was the journey to Naples, and all that is worth seeing in the city and its bay and Vesuvius, and the infinitely beautiful neighborhood. The fear of robbers did not prevent our seeing Pæstum and the remains of the old Greek temples. The seat of trade and most extensive commerce for some centuries in old Pæstum would have rewarded us for travelling any road, and we reached it by the most beautiful road in Europe.

CHAPTER XIV.

FOREST TREES: AN ADDRESS TO COUNTRY LADIES.

THE forest is commonly regarded as of value, because it affords materials for ship-building, for domestic architecture, for fuel, and for various useful and ornamental arts. But there are higher uses of the forest. More precious than the useful arts and more beautiful than the fine arts is the art of making home happy, — happy for children and wife and friends, happy for one's self, where all the wants of our nature may be gratified and satisfied, — not only those which belong to the body and the mind, but those which belong to the affections and the spirit, — not only the want of food and clothing and shelter and the other material wants, but those which are brought into existence by our love of the good and the beautiful. In every Christian home these tastes should be cherished as sources of deeper and serener happiness, more real, more permanent, and more independent of the freaks of fortune than anything which mere money can procure. Of the materials for building this happy home, next to those charities and graces which spring from the principles of the gospel and are nourished by the side of the domestic altar, next to that art of conversation which is the most precious fruit of a cultivated intellect and the source of unbounded delights, and to that love of reading which opens all the treasures of knowledge and wisdom to him who has it, — next to these, and their proper companion and complement, is the love of the beautiful in nature.

Nothing furnishes a larger, a more varying, or a more unfailing gratification to· this love of beauty than the forest, and the New England forest is far richer than that of any part of Europe north of Italy. At all times the forest is full of exquisite beauty ; and the forest and the garden are the schools in which the first lessons in the perception and enjoyment of beauty are to be learned. The cultivated fields, alternating with wood and mowing lands and pastures, orchards and gardens and dwelling-houses and barns, herds and flocks, the colors and shapes and motions of birds, — how beautiful ! And with what infinite beauty are fraught the changing clouds, the sky with its deep expanse of blue, the colors going and coming, varying from morning till night, the purple mists on the hills, the coming on of twilight and darkness, with its hosts of stars, — what a loss to every creature capable of this never-ceasing, exhaustless enjoyment, what a loss not to have the capacity awakened !

A capacity for the enjoyment of this beauty is nearly universal. By cultivating it we shall awaken a susceptibility for the higher moral and spiritual beauty which also everywhere is near us. I suppose that nature's beauty was intended to train the eye and the heart for this higher.

The sources of beauty in the forest are inexhaustible. Each mass of trees of one kind is an element of dis-

tinct and separate beauty. Each has its own shape,
its own colors, its own character. How unlike in all
these particulars are an elm and an oak! Not less
unlike are two forests made up chiefly, the one of elms,
the other of oaks.

Nearly allied to the elms, when seen in masses, are
the ostrya or hop-hornbeam, the carpinus or hornbeam,
and the celtis or nettle-tree and hackberry. Of the
same character with the oaks are the chestnuts, and
somewhat nearly, the beeches. But how different is a
mass of linden-trees! Entirely unlike each of these
and each other are the birches and poplars, when seen
growing together in numbers ; the birches grading down
with alders, on one side, and connected by the ostrya
with the oaks, on another.

A different element of landscape beauty are the willows, and a still more different the tupelos. A grove
of liriodendrons or tulip-trees has an aspect quite different from that of any other forest trees.

The pines, wholly dissimilar in their effect from any
of the trees with deciduous leaves, form among themselves several groups as unlike each other as the elms
and the oaks. The true pines, the pitch pine, the white
and the Norway, form one strikingly natural group. Yet
how unlike are the separate members ! How different
the appearance of a forest of pitch pines and of one of
white pines ! The larches form another group not less
distinct; the firs and spruces, another ; the cedars and
arbor-vitæs, another, and the hemlocks, more beautiful
than all, still another.

We see the cause of these different effects when we
come to study the individual trees. What an image of

strength and majesty is an oak! An old chestnut
hardly less. In the beech the character is softened into
a kindly, domestic beauty. A beech, with its clean
bark and rich, lasting leaves, glistening in the sun's
light, should be near a home for children to play under'
and women to admire. What majestic grace in the
American elm, whether it spread abroad its arms in
a gradual upward curve, bending down again at their
extremities and almost reaching the ground, forming
deep, vaulted arches of shade, or whether it rise in an
unbroken column to seventy or a hundred feet, and
there form an urn-shaped head, or a Grecian cup, or a
light, feathery plume!   ·

With what queenly stateliness rises the hickory, left,
by the native taste of the proprietor, in some green
field sloping down to the Nashua in Lancaster, or on
some other pleasant stream of the Atlantic slope in
New England! Of the four or five species of this
beautiful tree a natural group is formed, interfering
with no other, and including in its outer limits the
black-walnut and the butternut, by which it is allied in
its characteristics to the oaks, though still so remote.

The maples, giving their peculiar splendor to our
mountains and river-sides, would form still another alli-
ance. The rich colors of their spray in the early
days of spring and of their leaves as they ripen in
autumn are not its only claims to admiration. What
hopeful vigor in the aspiring trunk of a young rock-
maple! What dignity in the loftiness of the ancient
tree!

I know of nothing more delicately graceful than the
pensile spray of the fragrant birch, whether decked

with its golden catkins in April, or its light-green leaves at midsummer. So the silvery flash from the stem of a yellow birch, how charmingly it mingles with the lights and shadows of the depths of a forest! How startling, almost, is the effect of the gleam of white light from the bark of the canoe birch or the white or gray birch, in the same situation!

How magnificent the vast, columnar trunk of one of the few old plane-trees, or button-woods, which some unexplained disease or plague has left us!

What beauty is there in the manner in which the climbing plants, the drapery of the forest, are disposed! The trunks within the wood are occupied by a great variety of closely adhering epiphytes, lichens, which form upon the bark a thin crust or a delicate mossiness, or a brown, orange, yellow, or white star, — a study of themselves. The lichens which invest the bark of our birches, beeches, maples, and some other trees in the interior of the forest, are very curious. They seem, like strange Oriental writing, to have been formed by a delicate pen or brush, or a still more delicate graver. Such are the opegraphas. Not less beautiful are the finely dotted or stippled lecideas, lecanoras, and the starlike parmelias.

But on the edge of the forest, where the sun gets in, the climbers arrange themselves, like a curtain, to shut out the glare of day from the awful silence and sanctity of the deep recesses of the wood.

Where rather than in the forest are the simplest elements of beauty — color, form, and motion — to be studied? In the spring, every tree has its own shade of green, and these shades are changing, day by day and hour by hour, till they pass into the full, deep greens of summer, and thence in autumn into the rich reds, yellows, scarlets, crimsons and orange tints of the maples, tupelos, oaks, and birches, the purples and olives of the ash and beech, and the browns and buffs of the hackmatack, the hickory, and the elm. Not only the leaves, but the branches and trunks of all the trees have colors, — neutral tints, of their own. The forms are not less various, nor the motions, from the shivering of the leaves to the swaying and balancing of trunks and branches in the wind, — to say nothing of the colors and shapes and motions of birds and other animals best seen in the forest, with the reflected images in the lakes and streams. The combination of trees, and their contrasts in shape and character, their position on a plain or on the slope or summit of a hill; broad masses upon the side of a mountain, or covering its top, with wide or narrow glades losing themselves in their depths, and the play of light and shadow, in the sunshine or under a cloudy sky; the interchange of cultivated grounds and wild woods, and the grouping of trees, are circumstances by the study of which the student may be prepared to understand and to enjoy art as exhibited by the painter or the poet, as well as by the landscape gardener.

Sir Uvedale Price would have us study the works of the painters to form just ideas of the beautiful and the picturesque in scenery, — a pleasant study doubtless for those who have the means. But why not rather study the elements of beauty where Claude and Poussin and Salvator Rosa studied, in the forest, by the lake or waterfall, and by the sea? To the originals or to copies of the great paintings we may not easily find access ; but the originals of the originals are within reach of all of us.

Where else but in the forest did Shakespeare get that wild-wood spirit which makes us feel the airs and the very sounds of the woods breathing about us in "As You Like It"? Where else but beneath the "verdant roof," under "venerable columns,"

or in
> "Massy and tall and dark,"
>
> "Quiet valley and shaded glen,"

does Bryant refresh himself with pictures of early years, and forget

> "The eating cares of earth"?

The forest thus affords us inexhaustible means of giving variety and beauty to the face of the country ; and every person may avail himself of them from him who owns a single acre to him who has a thousand.

The planter is a painter on a vast scale, with the plains and slopes and hills of a township or a county for his canvas, all the colors of vegetable life for his tints, and real clouds, real rainbows, and real rocks, streams, and lakes for his background. Every tree has not only its own shape and outline, but its own shades and colors, always preserving the same general character, but varying in its hues and tintings from earliest spring to latest autumn, and yet with an undertone fixed, or but slightly changing, through the year.

Every mass of trees, of one kind, has the shapes and colors of the individual tree intensified by grouping, and brought into strong relief by brighter lights and deeper shadows.

The painter has thus for his pallet fifty marked and decided colors, with the power of modifying each by the introduction of any one or of any number of all the rest; and combined with these leading and substantive features are the forms and colors of all the numerous vines and climbers of our woods, which are continually modifying the impression of the branches and of the outline, — the lichens which spot or shade the trunks with colors gay or grave, the tracery of mosses, and the characteristic trailing plants and ferns which show themselves about the lowest part of the stem.

Of shrubs, he has a choice not less ample, both in color and shape, from the whortleberry, which rises a few inches from the ground, up through ledums, rodoras, andromedas, kalmias, sweet-ferns, candleberry myrtle, rhododendrons, azaleas, cornels, viburnums, dwarf oaks, the mountain and Pennsylvania maples, the glaucous magnolia, and how many others, till the imperceptible line is passed which separates shrubs from trees.

To each point in the picture he may give the color, the prominence, and the expression which shall most fitly belong to it, and shall best harmonize or contrast, with the recesses and projections, the forms and hues around. Much may be done to give breadth and extent. The apparent height of low hills may be increased by planting them with trees of gradually loftier stature, the summit being crowned with the tallest trees of the forest. To the perfect level of a plain may be given, by a similar selection, the appearance of an undulating or varying surface.

By the careful study of its character, every tree may be displayed to the greatest advantage. Spiry trees may be planted in the vicinity of steeples and other tall buildings, not to conceal, but to bring them forward; picturesque trees, with climbers and striking shrubbery, may be planted along steep slopes ; and quiet, round-headed, or drooping trees may clothe the low-lying sides of a lake or river. The various trees may be thrown into obscurity or brought prominently forward by their position in reference to roads and paths. These may be laid out so as to give the appearance, with the reality, of subserviency to mere convenience, or, when leading up into the woods, to favor the impression of wildness and intricacy so pleasing to the imagination.

To get command of the materials for this form of landscape painting, the student must go into the forest, not only every day in spring, but he must go in midsummer and in midwinter, and every day of autumn. He must study in the open glades and in the thickets, and he must look at the forest at a distance. He must learn the peculiar character of each tree standing by itself, and of the trees of each species, as seen growing together in masses ; and he must watch the effects produced by the combination and various grouping of the several trees ; how they are affected by the vicinage of rocks and of water, and how by climbing vines, fantastic roots, and other accidents of landscape.

Consider for a moment the changes which will take place in a forest just planted. Suppose that it occupies the summit of a hill and runs along down its side, accompanying the path of a brook, which is known formerly to have had a voice of music through the year, but which has, of late years, failed to be heard, from the improvident felling of the trees which once covered the hill. We have had it planted with larches and other deciduous trees and with evergreens; and we hope to live to see it make a conspicuous figure in the landscape. For the first few years it is beautiful chiefly to the eye of hope. The fences or hedges intended to screen the young trees from the sun and winds are the most prominent objects. But even in these earliest years, a walk to the hill will be well rewarded by the sight of the visible progress which many of the young nurslings have made. Every spot unusually protected or unusually moist will offer points of emerald green more beautiful and more precious to the eye of the planter than jewels. In the autumn, some of these spots will send out a brilliant gleam of scarlet or orange or purple.

In a few years more — a strangely short time — some of these trees will be distinctly visible at a distance, at all seasons, and will assume an individual character. They will overtop the fences and attract and fix the eye. The little rill will prolong its winter life further and further into the spring and summer. Its windings will be marked by greener grass and more flourishing young trees, and by the wild flowers which will have gone back to their native haunts, and the eye will glide pleasantly along its course to a river, or till it is lost in the distance. The outline of the hill will be changed from a tame, monotonous curve into one fringed and broken with inequalities, becoming every year more decided. The hill itself will become taller, wilder, and larger; and the forest, of which only the nearer side

will be seen, will stretch in imagination over distant
plains and hills beyond the limits of vision. The
stream will have resumed its never-ceasing course, and
the naiad her continuous song. The fences will have
become long since unnecessary and will have disappeared, and the sun's light will lie upon a sheltered
field by the edge of the wood. Pains have been taken,
in planting this hill, to avoid straight lines as the limit,
and to let deep angles, securing sheltered lots favorable
for tillage, cut into the forest. This, as the trees come
to maturity, will allow the eye to penetrate into these
pleasant nooks between woods on either hand.

The kinds of trees best suited to forest planting will
depend on the object the planter has in view. If that
be ship-timber, for a future generation, oaks, pines,
and larches will be planted, native and foreign. If his
object be to furnish materials for domestic architecture,
he will plant trees of the various tribes of pines. If
it be materials for furniture and the arts, he will plant
maples, birches, walnuts and hickories, lindens, alders,
ashes and chestnuts, beeches, willows, cherry-trees and
tulip-trees. If his object be the beauty of the landscape, he will plant or sow all the species of our native trees, shrubs, climbers, and under-shrubs, — oaks,
ashes, tulip-trees, chestnuts, birches, with various kinds
of pines and hemlocks upon the heights; elms, plane-
trees, pines, and some of the poplars on low hills or
parts of the plain to which seeming elevation is to be
given; lindens and walnuts, the black, the European,
and the butternut, upon the slopes; alders and willows,
tupelos and river poplars, the red and the black birch,
the white cedar and arbor-vitæ, along streams; the

cherry-trees and thorns, the several species of cornus, locusts, robinias, gleditzias, and acacias, elders, wild pears, and wild apple-trees, and whatever else has showy blossoms, along the edges most fully presented to view; birches, hornbeams and hop-hornbeams, the nettle-tree and the hackberry, elms of all kinds, poplars, native and foreign, beeches and ashes, pines and other evergreens, maples and oaks, everywhere.

Important questions, and worthy of careful and mature consideration, are, What trees are best suited to ornament the lawn; what best to be near a dwelling-house, where a family wants one tree, or a few, for beauty and shade, but has not room for many? What should be left or planted in pastures, for the comfort and health of sheep and cattle, and what are most ornamental and most suitable for public squares, large or small, and what for the sides of a road in the country, or a street in a city or town?

Every tree is more or less beautiful. Every tree is a picture, varying in color, in freshness, in softness or brilliancy, in light and shade, in outline, in motion, in all the accidents of vegetable life, through all the seasons and all the hours, from the beginning to the end of the year. Every long-lived tree of the taller sorts, such as oaks, elms, beeches, ashes, pines, may become a picture for many generations of the children of men,— a precious heirloom full of pleasant associations, and hallowed with the memories of parents and grand-parents, or of children early lost or long gone away never to return.

Every species of tree has its own peculiar inhabitants. Each is the favorite resort of particular birds, which prefer to build their nests in it, or if they build elsewhere, like to come and sing in its branches. Each species has its own insects, beautiful and friendly, or hostile ; its own epiphytes and parasites, lichens on its bark or dependent from its branches, and mosses and fungous plants which live upon its trunk or on its leaves in health or in decay.

The grandest of trees, in our climate, is the oak, and none will more generously repay every care which is bestowed upon it, or more surely carry our remembrance down to future generations, as it is the longest lived. There are many different species in America, all distinguished for different excellences. There are twelve well known as growing naturally in Massachusetts, and there are probably others ; certainly there are others in New England. Several from the West of Europe thrive here, and doubtless many from Asia, and from other parts of America, would grow well here. Our native species deserve our first attention.

The most valuable for the forest and the most magnificent for the lawn is the white oak, nearly allied to the European white oak. For the lawn, therefore, it is first to be chosen. The objection to the white oak as a roadside tree is, that it takes up too much space ; when allowed to grow unrestrained, it stretches out its vast arms to too great a distance on every side. We want, for roads and streets, trees which will afford shade, but which will lift up their arms out of the way. If we take an oak, it must be the chestnut oak, or the rock chestnut oak, or the scarlet. If we take an elm, it must be, for narrow streets, the English elm. The white oak is admirably suited, better than any other

8

tree, to the corner of a common, or a point where three roads meet at a large angle. In such a situation it will be able to develop its sublime qualities, and, in a century or two, will become the most venerable natural object in the county.

The red oak becomes a very large tree, grows rapidly, is very hardy, makes a fine head, has large, brilliant leaves, and a trunk which retains its youthful appearance very long.

The scarlet oak is a middle-sized tree, which recommends itself by its deeply cut and delicately shaped and polished leaves, and the rich colors they assume in autumn. There is no stiffness about the tree, and every individual of a long row would have its own shape and outline. This, however, is true of all the oaks.

A tree, found in the southern part of New England, in Massachusetts and Connecticut, and which recommends itself strongly by its size, its port, and the beauty of its leaves, and its large acorn-cups, is the over-cup white oak, seldom seen and therefore little known, but well deserving to be introduced everywhere upon the lawn or along the roadside.

The post oak is a small tree of some beauty, remarkable for the star-like shape of its leaves.

Some of the European oaks are worthy of cultivation; the two varieties of the English oak, both of which grow perfectly well with us, and the Turkey oak, nearly approaching to an evergreen.

It is not necessary to say a word about the American elm. Everybody knows it, and it is the only tree that most people do know. It speaks for itself.

The tulip-tree unites many qualities as an ornamental tree. It is beautiful when young, from the agreeable color of its bark, and its large, peculiar leaves. It is a rapid grower. It rises to a great height, and has fine, showy flowers and fruit, and it is wholly unlike all the other trees of our forest, — the only one of the magnolia family large enough to make much show.

A more picturesque tree, in its old age, very oak-like in its character, is the chestnut, which is hardy, grows more rapidly than most deciduous trees, and has a splendor of vigor and life scarcely surpassed. Its masses of starry yellow blossoms are conspicuous in summer, long after the blossoms of all other trees have disappeared.

The hackberry, when in perfection, has almost the grandeur of the oak, with something of the grace of the elm.

The Norway maple, and that which we get from England, where it is called sycamore, are valuable trees. The former stands against the northern blasts and the sea breezes better than almost any other tree. All our American maples should be seen on the lawn. They are unsurpassed in brilliancy and variety of color in autumn. The red maple, and the river or white, have too decided a tendency to spread, to be highly recommended for the sides of streets and roads. The rock maple is the best and finest of the tribe. It soars to the loftiest height, and wants nothing in shape or variety and brilliancy of color. It grows perfectly in a clayey soil.

The beech is perfectly well suited to stand near a house. It is always beautiful, has a clean stem, and bright, polished, glossy leaves, glancing spiritedly in the sun. It comes out early and retains its delicately colored leaves very late, and has showy blossoms and sweet nuts. It is said not to attract the electric fluid, and therefore is not struck by lightning, and is not as liable as most trees to be browsed upon by cattle. These two last qualities recommend it as particularly suitable to be planted in a pasture. Humanity, not less than enlightened economy, requires that shade be provided for the herds and flocks in their pastures. A few beeches, beautiful to the eye, will shelter them from the sun, and invite them to repose, instead of wandering. Other trees adapted to this purpose are lindens and maples. Beautiful pasture trees are all the species and varieties of the hickory. In deep soils they get much of their food from a point below the roots of the grasses, and therefore interfere little with a mowing field or pasture. They are also well suited for the sides of roads, as their tendency is not to form large lower limbs. They are thought to be peculiarly difficult to transplant; and so they are when taken from the forest or its neighborhood, but when properly managed in a nursery, their tendency to depend almost entirely upon the tap-root being corrected by judicious pruning of the root, they may be removed as safely as any other tree.

Would it not be worth while to take some pains to propagate more extensively a tree which bears so valuable a fruit as the shagbark?

Among middle-sized trees may be mentioned the sassafras, recommending itself by its curiously lobed, sweet leaves, its blossoms, and its striking fruits; the hornbeam, for the fine color of its fluted trunk and its handsome leaves ; the hop-hornbeam for the softness of its foliage ; the locust, not always a low tree, for its soft, satiny leaves, and fragrant, showy flowers, and the endless variety of its outline.

As in proper keeping with the regularity of a street, we may choose trees of regular and somewhat formal and monotonous beauty, such as the linden, and, when there is room enough, the horse-chestnut, or the red maple, or the river maple.

Many people, with a sentiment for beauty, but with little cultivation of taste, are delighted with mere symmetry in a tree. To such persons, a row of lindens will give great pleasure, on account of their symmetrical regularity, while the depth of shade and of color, and the fragrance of the blossoms of the English tree, recommend it to all.

The black-walnut and the butternut are sometimes planted for their fruit along enclosures, so as to serve, at the same time, for shade to travellers. Both these and the European walnut might be planted for these purposes still more extensively. They are all shade trees ; and in comparison with other nations of equal intelligence, we value too little the pleasant additions which the fruits of these trees make to the dessert, and to the economical produce of those who cultivate them.

The wild black cherry unites in a remarkable degree all the qualities which should recommend it for the forest, the lawn, and the avenue. It is a hardy, rapid grower, of shapely trunk and beautiful bark, leaves, and flowers ; it bears a valuable fruit ; its wood is hard and durable, and suited at once to the uses of the joiner and the cabinet-maker ; and it is so attractive to many insects as to draw them away from the more valuable fruit trees. Yet it is improvidently destroyed wherever it is found growing, from a belief that it actually creates injurious insects. It *seems* to do this only because it draws them away from the trees of the orchard, and concentrating them, gives the cultivator the opportunity of destroying them at once on one tree.   •

Few people have ventured to plant pines as shade trees on the sides of roads. The white pine is, however, well suited to this purpose. It is a rapid grower. Its lower branches may be removed with safety, and it has a fine, symmetrical head. One of the most imposing rows of trees I have ever seen in this country is a row of tall old white pines in North Berwick in Maine. When all its branches are permitted to grow, the white pine furnishes a better protection against the winds in winter than any deciduous tree.

When there is room for them to grow to their full development, several of the firs and spruces, and the common hemlock, are excellent for roadsides. But they must have ample space, as their beauty is destroyed by cutting away the lower branches.

The various species of nyssa, pepperidge, or tupelo tree have rarely been cultivated as shade trees or for ornament. Yet no other tree in our forests has such resplendent leaves ; none is so brilliantly green in summer, and none is more vividly scarlet and red and purple in autumn. And in its port it is altogether peculiar. Its fault is that its leaves fall early, and its brilliancy is transient.

The attention of cultivators has been so exclusively

fixed upon the valuable properties of the thorns as hedge plants, that they have often failed to perceive or to recognize their great variety of beauty for the lawn.

In Scotland and in the northern continental countries of Europe, the beauty of the birch is felt and has often been sung. The poorest of our birches is almost as good as the European birch, while the latter is young; and we have three others, all far more beautiful at all ages, the yellow birch, the black birch, and the canoe birch. They are unsurpassed in the delicacy of their outline, in the graceful sweep of their branches, in the vivid play of the sun's rays upon their leaves, and in the charming motions and colors of their pendulous flower-tassels in spring, at a season when most other trees give few signs of life. Tender and delicate as they seem, they are all singularly hardy, and swift and sure growers, even in the most exposed situations. The vegetable world does not offer a group of more graceful trees.

The plane-trees, Oriental and Occidental, or the European plane and our button-wood tree, form a pillar of vast size and strength, free from limbs near the ground, and admirably adapted to avenues and road-sides. In moist ground no other tree will make so conspicuous a figure. Its immense columnar trunk and large leaves took the fancy of the ancient Greeks, who preferred it above all other trees ; and the Romans in this, as in other matters of taste, followed the Greeks.

CHAPTER XV.

WHAT WE OWE TO LOUIS AGASSIZ AS A TEACHER.

An Address before the Boston Society of Natural History,
January 7, 1874.

MR. PRESIDENT : —

I THANK you for the great honor you do me by inviting me to say something before and in behalf of your
society, in ⁄commemoration of the most distinguished
naturalist that has appeared among us. You know
how reluctantly I consented to speak, and I feel how
inadequately I shall be able to represent the society.
Yet I cannot but admit that there is some apparent propriety in your request. I was one of those who formed
this society. All the others who first met are gone :
Dr. B. D. Greene, Dr. J. Ware, F. C. Gray, and the
rest, and my old friend, Dr. Walter Channing, in whose
office most of the first meetings were held. Moreover,
while I was in the· seat you now occupy, it was agreed
by my associates that it was very proper and desirable
that a survey of the State, botanical and zoölogical,
should be made, to complete that begun by Prof. Hitchcock in geology. At their request, I presented to Gov.
Everett a memorial suggesting this.

Our suggestion was graciously received. Gov. Ever-

ett brought the subject before the Legislature, in which
some friends of natural history in the House of Representatives had already been acting toward the same
end ; an appropriation was made, and he was authorized
to appoint a commission for that purpose. On that
commission four members of this society were placed,
the reports of three of whom, Dr. Harris, Dr. Gould,
and Dr. Storer, have been, and still continue to be,
considered of signal and permanent value, and Mr.
Agassiz himself regarded them as among the best
reports ever made. It has given and still gives me the
greatest satisfaction to know that the society has been
continually going forward, and that it is now more
prosperous than ever.

A little more than twenty-seven years ago, as I was
sitting in my study, a message came to me that two
gentlemen desired to see me. They were immediately
admitted, and Dr Gould introduced me to Louis Agassiz. His noble presence, the genial expression of his
face, his beaming eye and earnest, natural voice at once
gained me, and I responded cordially to his introduction. He said, " I have come to see you, because Dr.
Gould tells me that you know the trees of Massachusetts ; I wish to be made acquainted with the hickory.
I have found the leaves and fruit of several species in
the Jura Mountains, where they were deposited when
those mountains were formed ; but since that time none
have been found living in Europe. I want to know
them as they are now growing."

I told him that I knew all the species found in New
England, and should be glad to show them to him.
" But I have," I said, " presently to begin my morn-

ing's work.   If you will let me call on you immediately
after dinner, I shall be glad to take you to them."

At the time fixed I called on him at his lodgings,
and took him in my chaise, first to Parker's Hill, where
one species of hickory grew, then through Brookline,
Brighton, and Cambridge, where two others were found,
and to Chelsea, where a fourth and one that might be a
variety, were growing.   I pointed out the characteristics of each species in growth, branching, bark, fruit,
and leaves, and especially in the buds.   He listened
with the most captivating attention, and expressed surprise at my dwelling upon the peculiarities of the buds.
" I have never known the buds to be spoken of as a
characteristic," said he; " that is new to me."   He
admitted the distinct peculiarities of structure in the
buds, and I have no doubt remembered every word I
said, for, a few months afterwards, I saw in a news-
paper that Mr. Agassiz would give a lecture, in Rox-
bury, on the buds of trees.

We drove on to Chelsea Beach, which stretches off
several miles, apparently without end, and as the tide
was very low, was then nearly a quarter of a mile
wide.   He was charmed with everything, .expressing
his pleasure with all the earnestness of a happy child,
hardly able to restrain himself in his admiration and
delight.   He told me that he had never before been on
a sea-beach, but that he was familiar with the wave-
marks on the old beaches laid open in the Jura Mountains.

I need not say what a pleasant drive this was.   I had
long felt great interest in various departments of natural history, but had been so fully occupied with my own

duties as a teacher that I had been able to indulge myself fully, and that for a small part of the year, in one only. Here was a companion who was intimately acquainted with all, and with the most distinguished men who had been advancing them, and who was ready and happy to communicate wealth of information upon every point I could ask about.

Some days after, I invited all the members of this society to meet Mr. Agassiz at my house. Every one came that could come. They conversed very freely on several subjects, and Agassiz showed the fulness of his knowledge and his remarkable powers of instant observation. All seemed to feel what a precious accession American science was to receive.

Not long afterwards, Mr. Agassiz accepted an invitation to spend Christmas with us. We took some pains, ourselves and our children, among whom were then two bright boys, full of fun and frolic, one in college and one nearly prepared to enter. He was easily entertained, entering heartily, joyously, and hilariously into everything, games and all, as if he were still as young as the youngest, but full of feeling, and moved, even to tears, by some poor lines to him and his native land.

My friends, I have thus shown you how intimate I became, for a few weeks, with Agassiz, whom I found the wisest, the most thoroughly well-informed and communicative, the most warm-hearted and the most modest man of science with whom, personally or by his works, I had ever become acquainted. I did not keep up that intimate acquaintance, both because I was too busy in my own work, and because I did not deem

myself worthy to occupy so much of his time, consecrated, as it was, to science and the good of mankind.
The strong impression he made on me was made on
almost all who ever listened to or even met him. It is
not surprising then that the news of the death of Agassiz caused a throb of anguish in millions of hearts.
Such a death is a loss to mankind. What death among
kings or princes in the Old World, or among the aspi-
rants for power or the possessors of wealth in the New,
could produce such deep-felt regret?

He is gone. We shall see his benignant face and
hear his winning voice no more ; but we have before us
his example and his works. Let us dwell, for a few
moments, on some features in his life and character, as
an inspiration and a guide, especially to those who
mean to devote their leisure or their life to natural history, or to the great work of teaching. What a change
has taken place in the whole civilized world, and especially in this country, in men's estimation of the value
and interest of these pursuits, since he began his
studies. To whom is that change more due than to
Agassiz?

He was endowed by nature with extraordinary gifts.
His fascinating eye, his genial smile, his kindliness and
ready sympathy, his generous earnestness, his simplicity, and absence of pretension, his transparent sincerity, — these account for his natural eloquence and
persuasiveness of speech, his influence as a man, and
his attraction and power as a teacher. For the development and perfecting of many of his highest and most
estimable qualities of mind and character, Mr. Agassiz
was doubtless indebted to his noble mother, who, judg-

ing from everything we can learn, was a very rare and remarkable woman. To the quiet, homely, household duties, for which the Swiss women are distinguished, she added unconsciously very uncommon mental endowments, which she wisely cultivated by extensive reading of the best authors and by conversation with the most intelligent persons.

Trained by such a mother, Agassiz grew up in the belief of a Creator, an infinite and all-wise intelligence, author and governor of all things. He was sincerely and humbly religious. During his whole life, while exploring every secret of animal structure, he saw such wonderful consistency in every part that he never for a moment doubted that all were parts of one vast plan, the work of one infinite, all-comprehending thinker. He saw no place for accident, none for blind, unthinking brute or vegetable selection. Though he was a man of the rarest intellect, he was never ashamed to look upwards and recognize an infinitely higher and more comprehensive intellect above him.

In his earliest years and through childhood he was surrounded by animals, — fishes, birds, and other creatures, — which he delighted to study, and with whose habits and forms he thus became perfectly familiar. His education, in all respects, was very generous and thorough. He spent his early years in some of the most distinguished schools and colleges in Germany; and he had the good fortune to be made, early, a student of the two great languages of ancient times. He became familiar, by reading them in their native Greek, with the high thought and reasoned truth and graceful style of Plato, and the accurate observations and descriptions of Aristotle, the nicest observer of ancient times, and justly considered the father of natural history. Probably no work has been more suggestive to him than Aristotle's " History of Animals " ; and probably his own breadth of conception and largeness of thought, upon the highest subjects, were due, in no inconsiderable degree, to his early familiarity with Plato. He also read some of the best Latin authors, and wrote the language with great ease.

No one who early has the time and opportunity, and who desires to become a thorough naturalist, or a thinker on any subject, should neglect the study of these two languages. From them we borrow nearly all the peculiar terms of natural science, and find the originals of almost all the words which we use in speaking on ethical, metaphysical, æsthetical, and political subjects, and no one can be sure that he perfectly understands any of these words unless he knows them in their original language.

I dwell upon this subject, because I believe that the early study of language, especially of the ancient languages, is far too much undervalued. We use language, not only in our communication with others, but in our own thoughts. On all subjects of science, or whatever requires accurate thought, we think in words, and we cannot think, even within ourselves, upon any subject, without knowing the words to express our thoughts. He who is most fully and familiarly acquainted with the richest language and the thoughts that have been expressed by it, has the power of most easily becoming not only a good thinker, but an eloquent speaker. No greater mistake can be made, in the early education of the future naturalist, than the neglect to give him a full and familiar acquaintance with the words by which thought can be carried on or communicated.*

Agassiz's mother-tongue was French, but both this and German were in common use in the Pays de Vaud. He lived, for years afterwards, in several parts of Germany, and thus attained, without special study, the rich language which we Americans have to give so much time to acquire ; and he lived long, a studious and laborious life in Paris, where he became intimately acquainted with Cuvier and other distinguished naturalists, and perfectly familiar with the French language in its best form. More than once, when he was putting his note-book into his pocket, he told me he knew not whether he had made his notes in German or in French.

Agassiz's universality of study and thought suggests a precious lesson. It is never safe to give one's self entirely to one study or to one course of thought. The full powers of the mind cannot so be developed. Nature is infinite ; and a small part of one kingdom cannot be understood, however carefully studied, without some knowledge of the rest.

---

* It is a matter of the greatest satisfaction that the only true mode of learning language, the natural one, by word of mouth from living teachers, is becoming common; the language itself first, and afterwards the philosophy of it, — the rules. It is most desirable that this mode of learning the ancient languages should be introduced, to learn first the language, to read and understand it, and afterwards the rules. Indeed, I would not recommend the study even of Greek, if most or much of the time given to it had to be thrown away upon the grammar. The true mode, Agassiz's mode, of teaching on all subjects, is becoming more and more common.

Neither must a man allow himself to be a mere naturalist. Every man ought to seek to form for himself, for his own happiness and enjoyment, the highest character for intelligence, and for just and generous feeling, of which he is capable. He is not a mere student of a department of nature. He is a man; he must make himself a wise, generous, and well-informed man, able to sympathize with all that is most beautiful in nature and art, and best in society. It would be a poor, dull world, if all men of talent were to educate themselves to be mere artisans, mere politicians, or mere naturalists.

Agassiz took a large, comprehensive view of the whole field of natural history; his thorough education and intimate acquaintance with the works of the highest men in several walks, Von Martius, Cuvier, Humboldt, and others, made it possible for him to do it, and he then fixed on certain departments, and, for the time, he gave himself entirely to one.

As a future inhabitant of America, it was fortunate for him to have been born, and to have grown up, in one of the free cantons of Switzerland. He was thus accustomed to treat men as equals; and thus his perfect familiarity and his freedom from all assumption were as natural to him as they were graceful and winning. He looked down upon none, but felt a sympathy with everything best in every heart. The reality of these great human qualities gave a natural dignity which his hearty and ready laugh could never diminish. Every one was drawn toward him by what was best in himself. With the greatest gentleness he united a strong will, and with a resolute earnestness, untiring patience. His great object was truth, and as he never had any doubt that it was truth, he may have been impatient, but he never felt really angry, with those who opposed it.

Mr. Agassiz had, for several years, the great advantage and privilege of being an assistant, in the description and delineation of fishes from Brazil, to Von Martius, the genial and eloquent old man of Munich. In him he had the example of a man, who, with great resources as a naturalist, had, for many years, given himself, in a foreign country, to the study of a single department of botany, without, however, shutting his eyes to anything that was new and remarkable in any page of natural history. To one who was a good listener and never forgot what he heard, what a preparation must this have been for his own expedition, many years after, to the sources of the Amazon, to which he was invited by the Emperor of Brazil, in which he was assisted by the princely aid of his own friends, and from which he brought home a greater number of new species of fresh-water fishes than were ever before discovered by one individual, thus carrying forward that work upon the fishes of Brazil, his first work, which he had published when he was twenty-two years old.

He spent the leisure of several years in examining the reefs and dredging in the waters of the coast of Florida and other parts, always bringing home stores of new species and genera, and completing the history of innumerable known ones. What a preparation were these years for the great Hasler expedition, in which the depths of the ocean were very fully explored, and innumerable objects, new and old, were brought up, showing that the bottom of the ocean is anything but

9

barren, and throwing new light upon the geology of recent and of ancient times !

Whenever Mr. Agassiz undertook a special work, he prepared himself for it by a careful study of whatever had been done in that particular line by all others. He had seen everywhere indications of the action of ice. He determined to investigate. He began by reading all he could find upon the subject, and then set himself to observe, patiently and carefully, what was taking place in the glaciers themselves. He gave the leisure of several years to this examination, and then felt himself ready to observe the effects of similar action in former ages and distant regions. The opinions of such an observer, after such a preparation, cannot be without authority and value ; and it is not surprising that he should not himself have been willing to yield them to those of others who had never given the same study to the subject.

When he wrote his wonderfully complete work upon the American Testudinata, he began by studying whatever had been written in regard to that family of animals, and he furnished himself, by the liberal aid of many friends, with immense numbers of specimens, so that he had ample means of satisfying himself in regard to almost every question that could be asked as to structure * or habits. Such a work will not need to be done over again for many years. It can never be entirely superseded, except by a work showing greater diligence,

---

* In speaking of the thorough execution of the works in the four volumes, we ought not to forget the aid he received from the exquisite skill in drawing and engraving of Sonrel, who wore out his eyes in the work, and of Burckhardt and Clark.

greater fidelity, and better powers of nice observation and faithful description.

Let no one who has not carefully examined this, and his other papers in the " Contributions to the Natural History of the United States," venture to speak of his incompleteness.

His example as a teacher has been of inestimable value, as showing the importance of the best and largest possible preparation, teaching by things really existing and not by books, opening the eye to the richness and beauty of nature, showing that there is no spot, from the barren sea-beach to the top of the mountain, which does not present objects attractive to the youngest beginner, and worthy of and rewarding the careful consideration of the highest intellect.

The town of Neufchatel, near which Mr. Agassiz was born, and particularly the hills behind it, give fine views of natural scenery. From a hill, not two miles from his former home, I had a view of the lake and the plains and the mountains beyond, which I now recall as one of the widest, most varied, and most exquisite I have ever seen. Agassiz thus grew up to a love of the beautiful.

This love of the beautiful in nature has been increasing from the most ancient times to the present. It is more generally felt and more fully enjoyed now than ever before, and in this country, apparently, more than in any other. More persons leave the cities, as soon as they begin to grow warm and dusty, to enjoy the country or the seaside, the mountains or the lakes ; and they enjoy rationally and heartily. Who has done more than Agassiz to increase this enjoyment? With thou-

sands it is becoming not merely the enjoyment, but the
study of the beautiful. Collections of shells, curious
animals, minerals, sea-weeds, and flowers are becoming, like libraries, not only sources of pleasure to the
eye, but of delightful study, whereby a nearer approach
is made to the very fountain of enjoyment. We not
only see and feel, we begin to understand. The more
we see of the uses, of the wonders, of the structure,
the more profound is our enjoyment. Who has done
more than Agassiz to awaken this enjoyment?

In 1855, with the aid of Mrs. Agassiz, who, from the
beginning, did a great deal of the work, Mr. Agassiz
opened a school for young ladies. For this he was, in
all respects, admirably well qualified. The charm of his
manner, his perfect simplicity, sincerity, and warm-
heartedness, attracted every pupil, and won her respect,
love, and admiration. He knew, almost instinctively,
what we teachers have to learn by degrees, — that we
cannot really attract, control, and lead a child, and help
to form his habits and character, without first loving
him ; that nothing in the world is so powerful as real,
disinterested affection. He gave himself, by lectures
most carefully prepared, an hour's instruction, real
instruction, every day. All his pupils retain their
respect and love for him, and some keep the notes
they made of his talks, and read them with delight.
The school was continued for seven years, with great .
success, attracting pupils from distant parts of the
country.

One of the secrets of his success as a teacher was,
that he brought in nature to teach for him. The young
ladies of a large school were amused at his simplicity

in putting a grasshopper into the hand of each, as he came into the hall; but they were filled with surprise and delight, as he explained the structure of the insect before them, and a sigh of disappointment escaped from most of them when the lesson of more than an hour closed. He had opened their eyes to see the beauty of the wonderful make of one of the least of God's creatures. What a lesson was this to young women preparing to be teachers in the public schools of the Commonwealth, showing that in every field might be found objects to excite, and, well explained, to answer the questions, what, and how, and why, which children will always be asking.

He had all the elements necessary to an eloquent teacher, — voice, look, and manner, that instantly attracted attention; an inexhaustible flow of language, always expressive of rich thoughts, strong common-sense, a thorough knowledge of all the subjects on which he desired to speak, a sympathy with others so strong that it became magnetic, and a feeling of the value of what he had to say, which became and created enthusiasm. He thus held the attention of his audience, not only instructing and persuading them, but converting them into interested and admiring fellow-students.

His mode of teaching, especially in his ready use of the chalk and the blackboard, was a precious lesson to teachers. He appealed at once to the eye and to the ear, thus naturally forming the habit of attention, which it is so difficult to form by the study of books. Whoever learns this lesson will soon find that it is the teacher's part to do the study, to get complete possession of what is to be taught, in any subject, and how it is to be presented, while it is the part of the pupils to listen attentively and to remember. This they will easily do, and to show that they do remember, they may be easily led to give an account in writing of what they have heard. Every lesson will thus be not only an exercise of attention and memory, but a lesson in the English language, proper instruction in which is very much needed and very much neglected. Whenever a pupil does not fully understand, the teacher will have the opportunity, while he is at the blackboard, of enlarging and making intelligible.

Wherever the teacher shall be successful in adopting this true and natural mode of teaching, the poor text-books which now infest the country will be discontinued, and those who now keep school will become real teachers; school-keeping will be turned into teaching. When this method is fairly introduced, we shall hear no more of long, hard lessons at home, nor of pupils from good schools who have not learned to write English.

The advent of Agassiz is to be considered a most important event in the natural history of the country. The example of his character, his disinterestedness, his consecration to science, his readiness to oblige even the humblest and most modest, his superiority to self-interest, his sincerity and absence of all pretension, his enthusiasm in all that is noble, — all these recommended not only him, but the science he professed. Never was a life more richly filled with study, work, thought; and all was consecrated, not to the benefit of himself, but to the promotion of science for the good of his fellow-creatures.

For many years Mr. Agassiz has seemed to live only for the advancement of natural history, by the building up of his Museum, for which he had collected materials of the greatest possible diversity, which would, properly cared for and arranged, form a museum superior in numbers and variety to any similar collection in the world. Shall this great work be allowed to fail?

Let every person who honors the memory of Agassiz say, No! Let every one who regrets that the great main support of the noble structure is taken away, resolve that it shall not fail, but that, so far as depends on him and what he can do, IT SHALL GO ON AND BE BUILT AND FILLED, AND STAND FIRM, A GLORIOUS TEMPLE OF SCIENCE FOREVER.

CHAPTER XVI.

FAREWELL.

ON the day of parting, some of your number requested to be allowed to take a copy of what I had read, that they might send it to an absent friend, or keep it as a remembrance of me. I did not consent to this, from an unaffected feeling that what I had said was not worth so much trouble; but I promised to have it printed for them. As it passed through the press, I felt still more strongly than before how poor and inadequate is my expression of the great lessons I would fain inculcate. I beg you, therefore, not for a moment to judge of the value of these lessons from what I have written, but let my words lead you to the Divine source from which they are drawn. I beg you also to remember that this Farewell, though printed, is not published, and to use it, therefore, as if it were sent to you in manuscript.

THE hour has at last come, my dear young friends, when we must part. At the very moment when you have become more dear to me than ever before, when I feel that we more entirely sympathize, that you more cordially enter into my plans for your advancement, and that your progress is more satisfactory, at this moment we are preparing to separate. And it is right that it should be so. If we teachers have been able to do anything for you, it has been to prepare you to go on without our aid. We have never attempted to compel, we have hardly, indeed, attempted to lead you; but we have pointed out the objects which we have thought you ought to have in view, and have done what we could to encourage you to pursue them; we have presented the motives and inducements by which we have thought you ought to be urged, and we have endeavored to make them yours. This we have done with a profound conviction that all real progress must be voluntary, and that until we have enlisted your hearty co-operation in the work of your own education, we have accomplished nothing.

We have endeavored, every morning, to open to you some lesson from the words of the Saviour or his apostles, or those mighty, inspired men of old, whose language, ever since it was uttered, has furnished the fittest expression for the deepest wants and the highest aspirations of the human soul; expression of penitence and sorrow for sin, of prostration under affliction, of confidence and filial trust in that Father who alone can help, — the strong and unwavering confidence which a feeling of reliance on the strength of the Infinite Helper alone can give, and of the boundless hopes of immortality. We have endeavored to show you not only how comforting and necessary these words are to us, but how transcendently wise and reasonable. We have endeavored to teach you not only to say, with sinful David, " I am afflicted and ready to die," and " What is man that thou art mindful of him? " but with triumphant Paul, " I can do all things through Christ which strengtheneth me." We have done this, not only because we have ourselves daily felt the need of the instruction, the consolation, and the wisdom, which we find in these divine words and which we can find nowhere else, but because we have wished to do something to induce you, dear children, to form the habit of daily searching in these exhaustless treasures of wisdom and truth and love. And my earnest prayer to God is, that, if all the other lessons I have endeavored to inculcate shall be blotted from your practice and your memory, this at least may remain.

We have every day invited you to prostrate yourselves, with us, before the throne of mercy,' and to ask of God those things which are necessary for us. And this we have done not only because we have ourselves daily and hourly felt the need of support, strength, and guidance, which we believe God alone can give us; for, in reference to our special and personal wants, we would obey implicitly the command of our Saviour, " Enter into thy closet, and pray to thy Father in secret," but we have endeavored, in this also, to do something to form in you the habit of beginning every day and every work with asking the blessing of God. I believe in the efficacy of prayer. I believe that the sincere and heartfelt prayer is always heard; and, when it is a right prayer and offered in a right spirit, I believe it is always granted. How far we may pray for temporal blessings I know not. For myself, I dare not ask for anything temporal without adding, " Not my will but Thine be done." But for spiritual blessings, the only ones of any great consequence, we may pray without ceasing. Weak, frail, and tempted, as we are, we must pray; and however strong the temptation may be, I believe that if, in the moment of temptation, we can, in the spirit of Christ, throw ourselves into the arms of the Father and ask, Father, strengthen thy child, we shall obtain strength.

What, then, are the most important lessons which you
have been learning, or which you ought to have been
learning, during this preparatory course of discipline?
Is not the first so to use, improve, and occupy every
talent of body and of mind, every affection of the heart,
and every faculty of the soul, that they shall be at
least twofold greater and better than when they were
committed to you? Have you a right, on any other
condition, even to hope for those gracious words of
welcome from the great Master, " Well done, good and
faithful servant! enter thou into the joy of thy Lord"?

Is not the second, to set up a standard, in the improvement of·these talents, higher than anything earthly
can furnish, a standard which shall be made up from
your highest conceptions of what is best and most beautiful in the visible works of God, and of which you have
a model, in spiritual things in Him only who came in
the image of the Father? Is it not to aim continually
to be perfect, even as your Father in heaven is perfect?

Is it not your duty, in the third place, to devote all
these powers, thus carried as far towards perfection as
you can have strength and opportunity to carry them,
to the service of your fellow-creatures? To learn how,
in your sphere and according to your ability, to love
your neighbor as yourself?

And is not the highest and most. consummate and
comprehensive of duties, which the Saviour has repeated
as the first of all the commandments, to consecrate
yourselves, with all your powers of body improved by
obedience to his laws, with all your mental faculties
brightened and strengthened by the study of his works,
with all your social affections perfected by devotion to

his creatures, with all the capacities of your spiritual nature elevated by habitual reverence, by contemplation on his law and communion with him in prayer, to consecrate all to his love, to love the Lord thy God with all thy heart, and with all thy soul, and with all thy mind, and with all thy strength?

Think not that you are bound to forget or to sacrifice yourselves. On the contrary, the divine lesson of the talents *commands* us to cultivate and improve to the utmost *every* faculty we find ourselves possessed of. It only substitutes, for the selfish motives by which the man of this world is influenced, motives incomparably higher and stronger and more enduring. What higher motive for self-cultivation and self-improvement can we even conceive of than the hope of becoming more fit to be servants of God, fellow-workers with Christ, ministers of good to men?

Whatever faculty you find within you, do not fear to use and cultivate it to the highest degree. Whence, for example, is a love of the beautiful? Is it not the gift of him who is the Author of all of beauty that there is in creation? Can you hesitate to exercise the faculty he has given you upon the objects for which it was given? There are some among our fellow-creatures who are so constituted, or so educated, that they are to be won from evil only by their love of the beautiful. Study all forms of beauty and all means of expressing it. It cannot be useless to attempt to copy the beautiful shapes in which God has formed the works of his hand, or the colors in which he has clothed them.

If you live within reach of objects of natural history, do not let the opportunity be lost of studying them.

Study plants, birds, shells, rocks, anything that is
God's workmanship. Do not, for a moment, think
that the study of his works, pursued in a right spirit,
can fail to bring you nearer to him.·
Cultivate the power of expression. Study language.
The first miraculous gift to the earliest converts to
Christianity was the gift of tongues. It was necessary
for the highest service then ; it is not less so now. By
it we understand better, in proportion as we pursue the
study, whatever is said or written in our own language
or in other languages. By means of it we penetrate
intó whatever is the object of investigation, and set in
order our own thoughts and conclusions, and make
them clear and definite to ourselves. By means of it
only do we communicate to others, for their good or
pleasure or our own, our thoughts, feelings, wants,
purposes, and aspirations ; and we express them forci-
bly and effectually just in proportion as we possess
more fully, as we have cultivated more faithfully, this
wonderful power of expression. The extent of our
knowledge is measured, in some degree, by the extent
of our vocabulary. By nothing else is man so distinctly
raised above other animals as by the gift of articulate
language ; and by nothing else is one man so distinguished from another. The literature of a nation is the
expression of the thoughts, meditations, fancies, and
conclusions of the thinkers of that nation. Acquaintance with literature is an acquaintance with the minds
of which it is the exponent. The study of language is,
therefore, the most useful study in the preparatory
course of every one's education, and the study of general literature is, through life, one of the most delightful and profitable of human pursuits.

Our own English literature is, probably, taking all things into consideration, the richest of all literatures, and for us it is, without question, far the most valuable. I would therefore recommend to each one of you to make it a point to become somewhat fully acquainted with this noble literature. It will take many years. But the time, and you must devote only leisure time to it, will be well and most pleasantly spent; and in obtaining this knowledge you will necessarily become acquainted with the leading thoughts of the best thinkers, upon all the most important subjects, in morals, taste, criticism, history, philosophy, poetry, theology, antiquities, and philanthropy, that have occupied the minds of men. To have a great object like this in view will give a purpose to your reading, and will prevent its being desultory, though it may seem so.

There is a great deal of poetry in the language which is not worth reading. Of that, a compendium, such as Cleveland's, will furnish you with sufficient specimens. But there are great and noble poets with whom I would advise you to become familiar. Such are Shakespeare, Milton, Wordsworth, Cowper, Scott, Bryant, Gray, Goldsmith, Coleridge, Young, and Pope, especially the first eight or nine.

I regret that the course you have pursued on astronomy is so defective. For those who remain with me, I shall endeavor to remedy the defect. To all of you I would recommend a work by Mrs. Lowell, which is now in preparation, and two works by Prof. Nichol.

There are certain portions of history with which every well-educated person should endeavor to become familiar. Such are the history of our own country, of our mother country, of Western Europe in modern times, of Greece, of Rome, and of Judæa, which last you will best learn from the Sacred Scriptures.

I recommend to you, as valuable parts of your reading, books of travels and books of biography, as making you acquainted, better than anything else, with the world in which God has placed you, and with the occupants of that world. Biography tends to make us charitable. He must be thoroughly bigoted who shall continue to think ill of our brethren the Methodists, after reading attentively the life of Wesley; or to condemn in a mass those who belong to the Catholic Church, after having become intimate with the character of Fénélon. The life of Elizabeth Fry, or of William Penn, proves that there are earnest and sincere Christians amongst the Quakers; the life of Leighton shows that a bishop may be very humble, and that of Peabody or of Channing, that vital piety may dwell with one who rejects all authority of man's device, and admits that only of the simple Word of God.

We are all willing enough to believe in the piety, intelligence, and Christian faithfulness of those of our own sect: it is therefore particularly important, if we would make our reading help us to become charitable, in the comprehensive sense of charity, as explained to us by St. Paul, that we should seek to become acquainted with those who differ from us most in their theological opinions. There is no danger of our being made to waver in our own opinions, if we have formed them by prayerful study of the words of the Saviour; and if we have not, it is only right that we should waver, until we shall have learnt to obey that great command of

Christian liberty, "Prove all things, hold fast that which is good," and that higher command of the Saviour, "WHY, OF YOURSELVES, JUDGE YE NOT WHAT IS RIGHT?" He need not fear to be unduly biassed by the opinion of a brother who has thoroughly learnt the great lesson, "Call no man master on earth, for one is your master, even Christ, and all ye are brethren."

Upon the subject of morals, of moral philosophy, I have constantly referred you to the source of light and truth. It is profitable to read other books upon the subject, but it is dangerous to consider them as having authority. They may help us to think, to form opinions for ourselves, but every practical question must be settled by our own conscience, enlightened and guided by the truths of the gospel.

To the important subject of mental philosophy you have, in your course with me, paid little attention. This has not been from any forgetfulness or neglect on my part. The studies to which you have given your attention are more elemental and preliminary in their nature; and most of you are but just reaching the age at which metaphysics can be profitably studied. The time, however, is coming; and I can recommend as pleasant and useful books, "Reid on the Mind," "Stewart's Elements," "Locke on the Human Understanding," "Brown's Lectures on the Philosophy of the Human Mind."

As a help to careful reading and reflection, and to the storing up for use of what is most valuable, I would advise you to keep a diary, *not of your feelings*, but of the good thoughts or beautiful images which are presented or suggested by your observation, by your reading, or by conversation. This will cultivate your powers of expression, improve your habits of attention and observation, and strengthen your memory; and if rightly used, it will give you materials for improving and elevated conversation.

Conversation may be made the most delightful of all arts. Its first and necessary uses are to carry on intercourse in all the business of life, to communicate our wants, sorrows, feelings, affections, and purposes. It may be made an instrument to instruct, soothe, and delight. Too little is thought of it, and too little pains are taken to improve in it. Hence we find very few good talkers, where there might be many. Most people make no progress at all in it; they talk at sixty as they talk at sixteen. They say what comes into their mind, without reserve or selection, without choice of thought or of language. It should be managed much better; it may, by each one of you. A daily recurring opportunity of doing good to others by doing good to yourself, of contributing to the pleasure, instruction, and elevation of those nearest and dearest, ought to demand a better preparation. She who will take pains to have suitable topics for conversation, topics which will bring in narrative, imagery, witticism, sentiment, and will study the art of introducing them naturally and gracefully, will make herself a charming companion. and will be a blessing to the circle of which she is the ornament. Let me enjoin upon you to take pains in regard to your conversation, and let me remind you that the indispensable graces of a good talker are simplicity, naturalness, sincerity, and truth.

We have taken much pains, in the regulations of the

10

school, to induce you to form habits of punctuality and order in the disposal of your time. These you will find of the utmost consequence. After a few years, and as soon as you shall have entered upon the active duties of life, most of you will have very little leisure for reading or writing or private thought. That little will depend on your habits of order and punctuality, and will be of scarcely any avail, unless used with severe economy. But those few moments of leisure, `wisely used, will make the difference between thought-ful, well-informed, wise, and agreeable ladies, and friv-olous and gossiping old women.

There are two practical rules in reading which I would gladly engrave upon your memory. Be not deceived by names. A book with the best name — a sermon or theological treatise — may be the vehicle of arro-gance, self-sufficiency, bigotry, pride, uncharitableness, in short, of whatever is most inconsistent with, and hostile to, the very spirit of Christianity; while a ro-mance or a song may breathe the spirit of gentleness, humility, love, and charity, — the highest and peculiar graces of the gospel. Remember that he who began his prayer with thanking God that he was not as other men were, went away condemned.

The second rule is. remember that your heart, your imagination, your conscience, are in your own keeping. Whatever tends to stain the purity of your imagination, whatever tends to increase your pride and self-love, to make you think better of yourself and of those who agree with you, or to diminish your charitableness, and. make you think ill of others, of those who differ from you, whatever tends to diminish your love and reverence for God and his Providence, is bad and to be shunned, by whatever name it may be called.

I have spoken of some of the means you must use to improve the talents of which you will be called to render an account; and as all the parts of life are necessarily connected, I have naturally anticipated something of the uses to be made of the talents so improved. I shall not, of course, undertake to enter into all which is meant by devoting our talents to the service of our fellow-creatures. Every good life is necessarily devoted, directly or indirectly, to the service of mankind. We have before us, therefore, a subject as broad as human life, and as various.

To a single point in this wide field I would ask for a few moments your attention : it is the duty of educating yourselves for a life of charity, of devoting to charitable uses the talents you will have improved. I wish you to consider this question, whether it is not the duty of each one of you to prepare herself to do something effectually to relieve or diminish the wants, the ignorance, the sufferings, and the sins of her poor fellow-creatures? And by this preparation I mean something different from the general, vague, good purpose, which almost every woman has, to be charitable to the poor. I mean a special preparation, a careful inquiry as to what are the wants and what the condition of the poor, and what ought to be and can be done by Christian women for them. I should be most thankful to my Father in Heaven if I could know that he would move the hearts of many of you to choose this for your profession, as deliberately, as thoughtfully, and as resolutely as your brothers are choosing law, medicine, commerce, or some useful art. A great purpose for which Christ came on earth is not accomplished, the gospel is not yet preached to the poor; and I think it never can be until woman takes up the work. This need not take you from other duties; it will not interfere with them; for he who neglecteth to provide for those of his own house has denied the faith, and is worse than an infidel. It will only take time which would be otherwise lost.

You will ask me what I think you ought to do to prepare yourselves for a life of charity.

1. I would answer, the first requisisite is an earnest *desire* to engage seriously in the service of God, in the way which he has pointed out. How can you show this desire but by serving your fellow-creatures? How can you know that you love God, whom you have not seen, if you love not your brother whom you have seen? You cannot benefit God. He hath no need of you. All things are already his. You cannot *benefit* God. You can *serve* him only by serving your fellow-creatures.

Some of you will doubtless live a single life. Be not willing to lead a useless one. You will have the resources of art and taste, music, drawing, a rich and elegant literature, eloquent preaching and religious services that you delight in, refined and cultivated friends, pleasant homes, ample houses in city and country, and all the other appliances of wealth and luxury. And you can live very happy lives in the enjoyment of all these things. But can you, after hearing all the lessons of the gospel, *can* you suppose that a life so spent, no matter how innocently, no matter with how much refinement and elevation, that a life so spent for *self*, is a life acceptable to God?

2. The second requisite is, that you get a just idea of the greatness and excellence of this work, the true *nobleness* of a life of charity. What more noble work can there be, what more angelic, than to save from sin, from ignorance, from suffering, from despair? This is the life which the Divine Being who came into the world himself led. He was anointed to preach the gospel to the poor; he was sent to heal the broken-hearted, to preach deliverance to the captives, and the recovering of sight to the blind, and to set at liberty them that are bruised. Is not this a divine life? To be able to do either of these things, or to help in doing either, — is it not worthy of long-continued preparation and study? To do anything well requires time and labor. To cultivate roses successfully requires months of careful attention. To make skilfully a shoe or a bonnet requires months and even years of apprenticeship. To make well even the cheapest cotton fabrics which are worn by the poor has tasked the science, the ingenuity, the perseverance, the patience of many of the best thinkers. Is it worth a less expenditure of time and of thought to relieve the wants, to remove the ignorance, to cultivate the mind, to elevate the character of the wearer?

3. The next requisite and preparative is to search, studiously, the Scriptures. If with an humble, earnest, and prayerful spirit you consult these Oracles of God, light will come out of them to illuminate your darkness. We see lists of text-books and vade mecums for the lawyer, the physician, the architect, the engineer, and

we know that years are required to understand and master them. The text-books for the woman of charity are the Gospels, the Epistles, the Prophets, the Psalms. Are not these books worthy of equal study? They must be studied that you may fill your hearts with the spirit of these divine books, and that you may fill your memory with the precious words of consolation, encouragement, truth, hope, for your own support, and for the support and guidance of those to whom you would minister.

Read also the lives of eminently successful philanthropists. You can learn much by their experience, and your hearts will be warmed by their ardor. I do not recollect one of them who did not go about his or her work in the spirit of the gospel. When Elizabeth Fry went in amongst the abandoned women in the jails in London, she felt safe and sufficiently armed with only the Bible; and when Dorothy Dix goes amongst the felons and madmen in still more dangerous places in this country, her sole armor is the Bible, her trust, the Giver of the Bible.

4. The fourth requisite of which I shall speak is that you endeavor to live a holy life. Do the will of the Father, and you shall know of the truth; and I think none have a right to expect to be led into the truth except those who obey this condition. How can you know how to sympathize with the sorrows of others for sin, if you have never felt any sorrow for your own sin? How shall you be able to discern the deep wound of sin in another, if you have never opened your eyes to your own? How wilt thou see to pluck the mote out of thy brother's eye, when a beam is in thine own eye?

With these preparations, or, I should rather say, with this continual preparation, gird yourself to the great work. It is a great work, and yet, like all other great things, it is made up of little particulars. Each one of you is now, already, prepared to enter upon this work, at least, the apprenticeship to it. You can teach a poor child to read, or you can prepare her for the Sunday school, and use persuasions with her and with her parents to induce her to go there. You can teach the excellency of truth and obedience and honesty. You can teach the greatness and goodness of God, and his all-seeing presence. What you know already, you can teach.

What has been done to relieve the wants of the poor has often been unavailing, because it has been done in ignorance, — in ignorance of their character, wants, and circumstances. Will you not be willing to spend time in searching thoroughly into the wants, character, and condition of those whom you would relieve? It will take a great deal of time. True. What good thing does not? If you were not spending your time in relieving your poor brother, in what better way would you spend it? Would it be better to be reading the novels of the day? Will your sleep be sweeter when you have filled your imagination with the fancied sorrows of a fancied heroine, than when you have been endeavoring to teach a motherless child to follow the example of her risen Lord, to offer an evening prayer to her Father in Heaven? Would time be better spent in embroidery? Is a cushion or a slipper for your sister of more consequence than bread for a hungry child? Will your time be better spent in making and receiving calls? When you lay your head upon your pillow at night, and commit yourself to the protection of the watchful Shepherd of Israel, will it be a sweeter thought to you to enumerate the agreeable and fashionable people you reckon on your list of friends than to call to mind the lone and forsaken lambs you have been seeking to gather within His fold?

Will your time be better spent at the play, the opera, the concert, the ball, or in making preparations for them? Do not suppose, my dear children, that I condemn either of these; I do not. Indulge in them. Only take care to do it innocently. Take care not to neglect other things more important. Only remember that for all these things God will bring you into judgment. I do not condemn them; I only ask, When the sun shall be setting for the last time to your earthly eyes, which will sound sweetest to your memory's ear, the songs and airs of the concert and the opera, the merry tunes to which your own feet have moved, or the hymns in which you shall have taught poor outcast children to sing the praises of their God?

Oh, if you will try the value of time by an unfailing test, send forward your thoughts, on the wings of heaven-taught imagination, to that day when the Son of man shall come in his glory and all the holy angels with him, and before him shall be gathered all nations, and he shall separate them one from another; and the King shall say to those on his right hand, Come, ye blessed of my Father, inherit the kingdom prepared for you from the foundation of the world; for I was an hungered, and ye gave me meat; I was thirsty, and ye gave me drink; I was a stranger, and ye took me in;

naked, and ye clothed me ; I was sick, and ye visited me ; I was in prison, and ye came unto me. Then shall the righteous answer him, saying, When, Lord? And the King shall answer, and say unto them, Verily I say unto you, inasmuch as ye have done it unto one of the least of these my brethren, ye have done it unto me.

What will then be your rejoicing, if, while these words are uttered, a multitude shall present themselves before the King, of those whom you have fed and clothed, and saved from prison and ignorance and sin !

What will be your dismay, if, among all the recollections of earth, there shall not come one — *not one* — memory of a brother saved !

I have thus endeavored to suggest some of the means you are to use to cultivate the faculties which have been intrusted to you, and I have pointed out a great object to which you should devote them. I have endeavored especially to urge upon you the motives which should lead you to live a life of charity, and the great beauty and excellency of such a life.

I trust that the few words I have said will suffice to recall some of the many I have addressed to you in the daily morning lessons. I would only add that we must seek the means of obeying the first and great com · mandment, by giving ourselves resolutely and faithfully to the work which is suggested by the second, which is like unto it.